The
SECRET
TREASURE

The Castle Mystery Series

Dieter B. Kabus

The SECRET TREASURE

The Castle Mystery Series

Dieter B. Kabus

Here's Life Publishers

P.O. Box 1576, San Bernardino, CA 92402

The Castle Mystery Series
THE SECRET TREASURE
by Dieter B. Kabus

Cover illustration by Peter Pohle

Published by
HERE'S LIFE PUBLISHERS, INC.
P. 0. Box 1576
San Bernardino, CA 92402

HLP Product No. 951095
© 1985, Here's Life Publishers, Inc.
All rights reserved.
Printed in the United States of America.

Translated from the German
    Original Title: Funf Geschwister Auf Der
    Abenteuerburg
    © 1980 Verlag Schulte + Gerth   .

Library of Congress Cataloging-in-Publication Data

Kabus, Dieter, 1941-
    The secret treasure.
    (The Castle mystery series)
    Translation of: Fünf Geschwister auf der Abenteuerburg.
    Summary: With God's help and protection, five children vacationing
on the grounds of an ancient castle tangle with a suspicious doctor on
the trail of hidden treasure.
    [1. Castles—Fiction. 2. Buried treasure—Fiction. 3. Christian life—
Fiction. 4. Mystery and detective stories] I. Title. II. Series: Kabus, Dieter,
1941-   .Castle mystery series.

PZ7.K115Se 1985   [Fic]   85-8744
ISBN 0-89840-097-X

FOR MORE INFORMATION, WRITE:

L.I.F.E.—P.O. Box A399, Sydney South 2000, Australia
Campus Crusade for Christ of Canada—Box 300, Vancouver, B.C., V6C 2X3, Canada
Campus Crusade for Christ—103 Friar Street, Reading RG1, 1EP, Berkshire, England
Lay Institute for Evangelism—P.O. Box 8786, Auckland 3, New Zealand
Great Commission Movement of Nigeria—P.O. Box 500, Jos, Plateau State Nigeria, West Africa
Life Ministry—P.O. Box/Bus 91015, Auckland Park 2006, Republic of South Africa
Campus Crusade for Christ International—Arrowhead Springs, San Bernardino, CA 92414, U. S. A.

Table of Contents

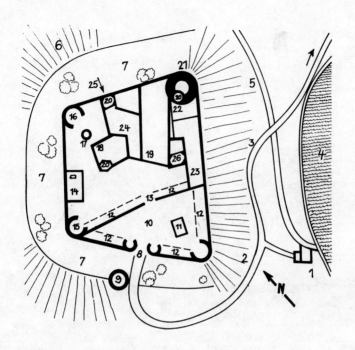

Ground Plan of the Castle

1. Old Mill
2. Steep slope
3. Road to the village
4. Lake
5. Brook with waterfalls
6. The castle hill
7. Deep moat
8. Drawbridge
9. Outer tower
10. Entranceway
11. Courtyard
12. Former farm buildings
13. Entrance to inner castle

14. Chapel
15. Western tower
16. Northern tower
17. Well
18. Residence
19. Knights' Hall
20. Stairway
21. High tower
22. Living room of castle
23. Outbuilding
24. Main building
25. Double wall
26. Stairway

The Discovery

The van cruised along the highway through southern Germany. Even with the windows open, the heat inside was stifling. When they had left that morning the five Baker children had been excited and full of plans. But now after seven hours of sitting in the warm van, everyone was unusually quiet. Fifteen-year-old Anne and the fourteen-year-old Rebecca were curled up asleep on their seats. To pass the time, Paul, thirteen years old, was playing a Bible quiz with his younger sister Katie. Eric, the youngest member of the family, was petting the Great Dane, Tawny, who was in her usual good mood, even though there was little room for her long legs and body. They had stopped often along the way to let her run.

"Hey, Mom, how much longer is it?" Paul asked.

"It can't be far now," Mrs. Baker answered. She sat stiffly at the steering wheel.

"I wish Dad could have come along," Eric said.

"So do I," replied Mrs. Baker. "He'll join us in two weeks." Their father, John Baker, was an American pastor, who was working for two years in Germany with Outreach to Youth. While he was at an important two week conference, he suggested the family take a special vacation. He had found an apartment for them in an old castle that now accepted tourists.

"Mom, is that the castle?" Paul asked, pointing straight ahead.

"I don't know," she replied. "I'd better look at the map."

Anne and Rebecca awoke as the van pulled to a stop under a clump of trees. "When are we going to get there?" Rebecca groaned.

"I think the castle just ahead is the one we're looking for," Mrs. Baker replied, unfolding the road map.

"Which one?" Katie asked, climbing out of the van, followed by the others.

Ahead of them, rising out of a misty hillside, stood a tall castle.

"It looks spooky!" Rebecca exclaimed.

"That's great!" replied Katie.

"I'm sure that's the castle we're looking for," said Mrs. Baker. "Come on, get back in the van. I'd like to get there before dark."

Now the children were excited and began making plans. Anne and Rebecca wanted to sleep in the next morning, but Paul and Katie wanted to lose no time in exploring the castle.

Just below the castle was a village where the Bakers were to pick up the key to their apartment from a woman named Frau Martin. They located her house, and Mrs. Baker knocked at the door. A friendly woman opened the door and led the family into her living room. Three boys were there playing guitars. As soon as they had been introduced, the boys — Andreas, Markus and Simon — left the room.

Eric whispered, "Did you see that? They have the same song books we have."

"Your apartment is in the courtyard of the castle," Frau Martin explained, "in a very nice old house."

"You mean we won't be staying in the castle?" Katie asked.

"No, but you may go into the castle," Frau Martin continued, "except for the rooms that are occupied. Of course, you must not damage anything."

"We didn't know anyone was living in the castle," Mrs. Baker said.

"There's a Professor Crippen living there. He is an art historian and works for the owner of the castle, Baron von Zerbach. Because the baron is seldom here and we are good friends, we keep the keys for the castle and the apartment," Frau Martin explained.

"Where does the professor live? What does he do?" Anne inquired.

"Well," Frau Martin hesitated, "he never talks about it, but the Baron told me that Professor Crippen offered to research and write up the history of the castle without charge. Because an older history already exists, the Zerbachs were not really interested, but finally the professor was allowed to stay in two rooms. Well, it will be dark soon. I think you'd better go on. If you have any further questions, call me. I wish you God's blessings for your vacation."

The Bakers were all surprised at this greeting, but Mrs. Baker recovered quickly and replied, "God bless you too."

In a few minutes they arrived at the castle. The gates to the entranceway stood open so Mrs. Baker could drive over the bridge and up to the front of the house.

The children were hardly out of the van when

Paul ran to the open gate to the castle's inner courtyard and stared in awe at the magnificent main building, the high tower, and the many smaller buildings. The other children hurried to him.

"Wow! Look at that tower!" Eric exclaimed.

Suddenly a heavy-set man appeared in one of the doorways. "Hello, I suppose you are the new guests," he said in English. "My name is Professor Crippen."

After the Bakers had introduced themselves, Rebecca asked, "Do you live here all the time?"

Frau Martin already explained that, Anne thought. *As usual, Rebecca wasn't paying attention.*

"Oh, no," Professor answered. "I've been here for only the last six weeks. Baron von Zerbach asked me to research the history of the castle. I told him about all of my work and how little time I have, but he insisted on paying any price to have this work done. So reluctantly I agreed to do the job." He pointed at one of the houses. "I live over there."

Anne thought, *Wait a minute. That's not what Frau Martin told us.* She studied Professor Crippen's face.

Aware of her penetrating glance, the professor turned toward the courtyard.

"Come on, children," Mrs. Baker called. "Please help bring the luggage from the van into the house."

"I'll be glad to help," Professor Crippen offered.

"Oh, good!" Rebecca exclaimed. "You can carry the heavy suitcases."

"Well, I suppose I could," the professor answered with a weak smile.

Anne was embarrassed and gave her sister a

warning look.

Undaunted, Rebecca continued. "We also have a dog in the car. When she stands up, she's bigger than you are. She hasn't had her dinner yet, so be careful!"

"Rebecca, what are you saying?" Anne scolded.

"Oh, that's all right," Professor Crippen answered. "I can see she likes to tease."

Paul opened the back door of the van, and the Great Dane jumped out. She sniffled her way over the wide courtyard. Professor Crippen eyed her cautiously. Then he helped carry the luggage into the house and showed everyone to their rooms.

As soon as the suitcases had been distributed to the proper rooms, the Bakers thanked him for his help. Katie, Anne, and Eric accompanied him to the front door. Outside, Eric noticed that the van door was open and tried to close it, but couldn't reach the handle.

Professor Crippen came to the rescue. "Let me help you." When the door was closed, he could see the sticker on the window: *JESUS, YOUR ONLY HOPE* stood out in huge letters. For a moment the professor frowned at the sticker, then turned to the children. "Good night," he snapped and hurried into the castle.

"Did you see the expression on his face?" Anne whispered. "That was strange."

"Yes," Katie replied. "He looked upset, as if the sticker reminded him of something."

Just then Rebecca called from a window. "Anybody who's hungry better hurry up."

Katie, Anne, and Eric hurried to the house. There Paul was busy setting the table. After dinner everyone was ready to go to bed early. Anne and Katie decided to share a room for the first few days.

Anne fell asleep almost immediately, but awoke some time later. Thirsty, she went to the kitchen and poured herself a glass of orange juice. As she was drinking the juice, she glanced out the window. Beyond the open courtyard gate she saw that a window in one of the buildings was dimly lit. *The professor is up awfully late,* she thought and looked at the travel alarm clock they had brought. It had stopped, so she wound it up and set it for twelve o'clock.

Yawning, she returned to bed. Before falling asleep, she realized that the dimly lit window could not be in Professor Crippen's apartment, because his rooms were in the wide wing of the main building. *Then who could it be?* she asked herself.

A Tour of the Castle

B ecause the next day was Sunday, the Baker family had a late breakfast. At the table Anne remembered her experience during the night and told the family about it.

"There's nothing unusual about that," Paul commented. "Lots of people work at night. What time was it?"

"Just a minute," Anne said, running to the kitchen, where the clock showed six. After glancing at her mother's watch Anne explained, "When I looked at the clock during the night, I noticed that it had stopped. I wound it and set the hands for twelve. Now it's six o'clock according to the clock, so that was six hours ago. Because it's nine o'clock now, it must have been three when I saw the light in the building."

"Good thinking!" said Katie. "I suppose it isn't unusual for a professor to work late at night."

Rebecca interrupted. "But there is something odd. Professor Crippen seems to have been lying when he told us about his work. Frau Martin told us an altogether different story."

"You mustn't judge a person negatively just on the basis of some feeling," their mother said. "I remember Frau Martin saying that she wasn't sure about the information. Perhaps she was mistaken and the professor told us the truth."

By the look on Rebecca's face Mrs. Baker could see that she wasn't convinced. "Straighten up your rooms and don't forget the table and the kitchen. We'll drive to church in a half hour. Meanwhile, I want to ask the professor if he can show us through the old castle. That will give you all a chance to get to know him better and forget your suspicions."

Professor Crippen agreed to guide the family through the castle, and after church they met him in the castle yard.

The professor began by giving them an introductory lecture on the history of the castle. At first, the children listened with interest, but after five minutes, they were bored. The many dates confused them and, it seemed, the professor as well, because their mother, who had listened carefully, had to correct him several times when he got his dates mixed up.

Finally, the doctor took a key from his pocket and unlocked the main door of the castle. They entered a large reception hall. The walls were paneled halfway up. Old cupboards lined the walls, and leather armchairs stood before an immense fireplace.

"Yuck! It smells musty in here!" Rebecca exclaimed.

"Old vacant rooms always smell like that," Professor Crippen answered with a smile.

After they had toured the ground floor with the kitchen and its many side rooms, the professor led them up to the next floor to the Knights' Hall. The children were impressed by the long heavy table with its forty chairs. A huge fireplace, decorated with a suit of armor on each side, dominated the room. Heavy velvet curtains kept the light out, so everything looked dark and sinister. On the wall across from the fireplace hung twelve large oil paintings, portraits of the castle's owners, dating from 1483 to 1823.

"What a huge grandfather clock!" Eric exclaimed, "Does it work?"

"No one is around to keep it wound up," Professor Crippen said. "But listen to the gong strike." He opened the door. Inside, the children could see weights and the pendulum.

Eric went closer to look into the clock. "There's a lot of space in it," he said. Everyone started in surprise as the heavy gong sounded and reverberated throughout the large room.

"Are we going to climb into the tower?" Paul asked eagerly.

"I can understand that you don't want to miss that," said Professor Crippen. "We can reach it from a nearby building. We'll go up there soon."

For another half hour, they explored more rooms and climbed several staircases. In one hallway, Rebecca said, "It smells better here."

"You're just getting used to the smell," Paul teased.

"So," Professor Crippen interrupted. "We'll be in the tower in two minutes. Because the dungeon is underneath, the entrance is on the third floor."

They finally reached the impressive tower, and the children ascended the winding stairs. On top they had a wonderful view.

"The town is way down there," Anne gasped, "How small those houses look!"

"Hey, check that out!" Katie exclaimed. "Right next to the castle moat is a lake!"

"Great! We could go swimming there!" Paul added.

Just then Professor Crippen came puffing up onto the platform. "This lake is approximately one kilometer long and half as wide. Now you've seen everything from here, and you're probably getting tired. Let's have a look at the chapel."

"I could spend the whole day in the castle!" Paul exclaimed.

"I'm sure, but I have work to do," Professor Crippen answered firmly. "Down in the courtyard there is plenty of space for games."

"Is there a cellar here?" Katie asked. "We didn't see one."

The professor ignored her question. He looked down at the castle with a seemingly preoccupied expression.

Eric repeated the question. "Is there a cellar?"

The professor looked at him and said, "You've seen a lot today, haven't you?"

"But no cellar," Eric maintained stubbornly.

When Professor Crippen noticed that everyone was staring at him, he said mysteriously, "Yes, the castle has a cellar—the dungeon!" Then he commanded in a stern voice, "Now let's go downstairs and look at the chapel."

The little church glowed with a festive atmosphere. At first the children were fascinated by the wonderful decorated winged altar. The large middle part depicted Christ's crucifixion. On the left wing were the shepherds kneeling at the manger, and on the right wing, the Wise Men from the East. Deeply moved, the children stood in front of the pictures.

Rebecca turned to the professor. "When was this altar made?"

"Late Baroque, about 1750, I would judge from the style of the building. But the pictures show some early Baroque elements of southern German school," Professor Crippen explained.

"Could this mean that they at one time belonged to another altar?" Rebecca inquired.

"That could be," Professor Crippen murmured. "But perhaps the painter was older and painted in an earlier style. Who knows?"

"Look at that Christ Child in the manger!" Anne pointed to the left wing. "It looks almost modern. The outstretched arms remind me of the cross."

A baptismal font stood at the entranceway to the chapel. On each side of the chapel were five rows of pews. The floor was made up of many flat gravestones. The walls were almost covered with similar stones.

"This chapel looks like a cemetery," Rebecca whispered.

Professor Crippen heard her. "In a way it is. There are certainly graves under the floor stones, but the stones on the walls are more likely memorial plaques for those who died in foreign countries and could not be transported home."

Warm air drifted in through the open door and drew everyone out into the sunny courtyard. Here Mrs. Baker and the children thanked Professor Crippen and began to walk toward their apartment.

Anne stopped under the archway, looked back, and said, "We didn't visit the part of the castle where the light was burning last night."

"Can you be sure of that?" Mrs. Baker asked.

"I'm sure," Anne insisted, "because I looked out of every window into the courtyard."

Mrs. Baker turned and walked to the apartment entranceway. The children followed and were greeted by Tawny's happy barking.

When they were all sitting in the apartment, Mrs. Baker said, "I think we should plan our schedule for the week. What do you think?"

"May I cook dinner tomorrow?" Rebecca asked.

"I want to cook too," everyone cried at once.

"Yes, yes," Mrs. Baker assured them. "You all may cook your favorite meal." After they had finished planning meals, they scheduled hikes, picnics, and other activities. They decided there still was time to walk around the lake and afterwards take a tour of the village, finishing up with a visit to an ice cream shop.

The path around the lake was well kept. Just below the castle the family discovered a very old and apparently vacant mill at the mouth of a large stream that reached the lake after passing over several water falls. In the middle of the lake was an island. Anne and Katie decided that they would cross over to the island on some warm day.

In the village there were many old houses, creating a quaint, peaceful atmosphere. Though they enjoyed the visit to the ice cream shop, the children were tired, and the walk back up the hill seemed longer than it was.

Trapped!

B ecause they'd made no specific plans for the next day, all the Bakers did what they wanted. Eric sat strumming dreamily on his guitar. Rebecca walked to the village, and Anne curled up with a book. Katie and Paul were eager to get a better look at the castle.

"I'd like to climb up there," Paul said, pointing to the castle wall.

"But how?"

Paul looked at some stones sticking out from the wall. "What about those? They look as if they had been part of an old building."

"Let's try it!" Katie's eyes were shining.

Climbing was easier than they had expected. Soon both children had arrived on top of the broad castle wall. Here the stones were cemented together, so people could easily walk on top of the wall.

At first their walk seemed to end at a bordering house. But then Paul noticed another wall, just half as wide, surrounding the house about two feet lower. Both children were surprised, because this lower wall had not been visible from the courtyard.

"Should we keep going?" Paul asked. "Maybe this wall leads around the whole castle."

Paul and Katie peered down at the tree tops, which seemed to reach up at them.

"Of course we'll keep going," Katie answered

and carefully slid down to the protruding wall.

Slowly both children crept along. The wall led them past several windows. After they had reached the corner of the house, they discovered to their disappointment that the castle wall ended about ten feet away. They decided to retrace their footsteps.

Paul grasped an iron bar for balance and accidentally nudged a small window with his hand. He looked up in astonishment. The window pane had opened slightly.

"Come here, quick," he called, and pushed the window open all the way.

Paul and Katie looked through and saw a staircase. They listened carefully, but heard nothing.

"Should we climb in?" Katie whispered.

"If we can. It looks too narrow," Paul said. "You try it first. You're skinnier than I am."

Carefully Katie pushed her body through the opening. "There's a door. I'll go and see what's on the other side of it."

Paul nodded encouragingly. "Maybe you can open the bigger window so I can get in."

The door swung heavily on its hinges. *It must not have been used for a long time,* Katie decided. The room beyond looked like a bedroom. A four-poster bed with long curtains stood in the corner. Paul knocked impatiently at the window. Katie opened it and helped him climb in. As they stood in the room, their love for adventure struggled with their conscience.

"There's nothing wrong with what we're doing," Paul said defensively.

"We're just having a look at the castle," Katie

agreed. "Nobody will care. Besides, the professor forgot to show us this part."

Curiosity led them farther. They walked to the staircase, climbed up to the next floor, and found a loft with a row of small rooms where servants might have slept. Above this was an attic filled with old junk. Because it was dark, the children did not enter, but descended the stairs again.

On the main floor was the kitchen and several smaller rooms. Katie looked out into the courtyard and saw Anne, Rebecca, and Eric near a well on the other side of the gate.

"Quiet," whispered Paul suddenly. "What's that?"

"What are you talking about?" asked Katie.

"Shh!" Paul put his finger up to his lips, "I heard something."

"Is somebody coming?"

"No, it was something else." Paul shook his head, thinking.

Then they both heard it: the wall reverberated several times with a hollow boom. The muffled sound was repeated at irregular intervals.

"Let's go find out what that is," Paul urged, although his face betrayed his own hesitancy.

"No, let's go back to the apartment."

Both Paul and Katie climbed through the larger window and shut it carefully from the outside. The other children were surprised to see them climbing down the wall.

"Have you been on the castle wall all this time?" asked Anne. They both shook their heads and acted secretive. But they couldn't keep quiet for long.

Breathlessly the others listened to the story of their adventure, looking up in awe at the old walls.

"We were over there to the left in that building," Paul reported.

"We weren't in that part on our tour," Rebecca said. "Did you see anything interesting in there?"

Paul shrugged his shoulders. "Not really."

"That's probably why the professor didn't show it to us," Eric said.

"That might be," agreed Paul, "but it doesn't explain the sounds we heard."

All five of the children looked puzzled.

"The best thing would be to sneak in after lunch and find out about those sounds," Katie suggested.

Because Rebecca was supposed to cook the lunch meal, and every one knew that this could take a long time, they all decided to help. Mrs. Baker noticed that the children were in a hurry, but didn't say anything. After the children had eaten and cleaned up, they quietly left the house.

A few minutes later, Mrs. Baker went outside. *Where could they be?* she wondered. They had even left the dog at home. Shaking her head, she reentered the apartment.

All five of the Baker children walked slowly along the top of the wall until they reached the window. When they all had climbed into the room, they listened in silence. Not a sound was to be heard. In hushed tones they conferred and decided to inspect as many rooms as possible in the hope of finding out what had caused the thumping. Unfortunately, the only door that led to the other building was locked. Disappointed, the five thought over what they should do and decided to inspect the attic. Paul offered to get the flashlight from the car. When he returned, they set out to investigate the attic.

The children found chests, chairs, lamps, weapons, parts of armor, tables, cupboards, pictures, and clocks. Suddenly their quiet search was interrupted.

"Hey, I've found a door that leads down," Rebecca called eagerly.

Without realizing it, the children had crossed from the attic of one house to the attic of an adjoining house. Instantly their eagerness to discover something new was again in full bloom.

"We've been in this building before," Katie said, "On the day the professor led us through the castle. If I'm not mistaken, the Knights' Hall should be in here."

She opened the big double door, entered, and bowing, announced: "Ladies and gentlemen, please enter!"

"There she is, showing off again," Paul muttered.

The children began by examining the suits of armor.

"I'd like to try one of those on," Paul said.

"That shouldn't be too hard," Anne replied. "All of the parts are connected with leather straps and buckles."

"I wouldn't try it," Rebecca warned. "Let's look at everything else first."

Paul seemed to go along with this suggestion, because he backed up and approached the huge fireplace. Eric had been admiring a five-armed candle stick when one of the candles fell to the floor and rolled under the table. He set the candle stick on the table and crawled on his hands and knees to look for the candle. On the underside of the table he found a space that was used to store extra table leaves when the table was made smaller. *A good hiding place*, Eric thought, and climbed in. "Hey, can anybody find me?" he called.

Katie, who had been standing nearby, heard him, bent down, and looked under the table. "Wow, that's a good hiding place!"

Suddenly from downstairs they heard a sinister sound. A key was turned in a lock, a bolt thrown back, and a creaking door opened. Anne motioned wildly to Rebecca, "Close the hall door!"

Rebecca tiptoed quickly to the door and closed it.

Holding their breath in fear, the children heard the door downstairs being closed and locked. A few seconds later the sound of footsteps coming up the stairs stirred the children to action.

"Over there's a door," Paul exclaimed. "Get in there, quick!"

It was the only way out of the room. Still under the table, Katie saw Eric's frightened look and whispered, "Stay here, you'll be safe!" Then she jumped up, hastily straightened the chair, and hurried to the others.

As soon as the door was closed behind her, she looked around the room and found that it offered no hiding place. Except for a pump, a stone basin, a bookshelf, and a long, narrow table, the room was empty.

Tip for map readers: This is the •stairway marked Number 26.

The footsteps continued slowly up the stairs. Paul felt his pulse hammering in his forehead. He looked toward Anne and saw that she was praying.

"It's our own fault," Paul prayed, "Lord, help us out of this mess!"

The footsteps had reached the second floor and moved to the door of the Knights' Hall. For an instant the children were relieved.

Suddenly Rebecca cried, "Where's Eric? Eric is missing!"

Anne waved her hands and placed a warning finger on her lips. Katie tiptoed to Rebecca and whispered, "He's sitting under the table—I mean in the table. He's all right."

Someone entered the Knights' Hall. The footsteps did not approach the door the children were hiding behind. Instead, they moved in the opposite direction. Then they stopped, a chair was moved, and again all was silent. Katie felt drops of sweat running down her face. Tense with anxiety, the children listened for further movement in the next room. It sounded as if the person was walking toward the front of the rooms. There was a *click*, then all was quiet.

Five minutes seemed like an eternity. The children waited, motionless. Ten minutes later—and still nothing. Slowly, the children relaxed. Paul looked at Anne and shrugged his shoulders. Katie crept to a second door, which led to a stairway, and slowly pushed down the handle. Nothing happened. She knelt and looked through the keyhole and muttered, "Locked from the outside."

Anne looked at Rebecca, her eyes wide with fear. "We're trapped!"

The Disappearing Man

P aul was the first one to find words. "Maybe somebody's there," he whispered to the others.

Anne shook her head. "There are only two doors to the Knights' Hall. If the person left, we'd have heard it. He could be sitting in a chair reading."

"Then we'll just have to wait until he goes," Paul said, and sat down on the floor.

Another fifteen minutes passed. Then a new sound awakened their fears. They stared at the door and saw the handle being slowly pushed down. Their hearts seemed to stop beating. Rebecca and Katie couldn't stand the tension anymore. They bowed their heads and closed their eyes.

"Eric!" Anne cried softly and immediately put her hand over her mouth. She pulled Eric into the room. She closed the door and asked, "Did you see him?"

"No," Eric answered. "All of a sudden everything was quiet."

"But that can't be," Paul objected. "The Knights' Hall—."

"Quick!" Anne interrupted. "Let's get out of here!"

Everyone hurried to the door and bounded down the stairs.

They closed the door to their apartment and sank

exhausted into chairs in the living room.

After she had caught her breath, Katie looked at Eric and asked, "Where did the professor go?"

"I don't know. I couldn't see anything."

"I can understand that," Rebecca sympathized. "At a moment like that, I'd have crawled under the table too."

"Who says that it was the professor anyway?" Anne asked.

"We could check up on him," Rebecca suggested.

"Oh, sure!" Paul said. "And what if he happens to be home?"

"Then we'll ask him some questions," Rebecca replied.

Once more the children felt adventurous. They hurried to the building where the professor lived. They opened the door into a narrow hallway and looked around. On the first door they found a nameplate that said, "Professor G. Crippen." An arrow pointed to a door knocker. Underneath, a sign read: "Please knock here."

"Go ahead," urged Katie, "knock!"

"What should I say?" Paul asked, wanting to be cautious.

"Ask him if we can go back to the tower," Katie suggested.

Paul nodded and lifted the door knocker and then dropped it.

Everyone jumped at the heavy boom of the knocker. For a few seconds nothing happened. Then they heard Professor Crippen's voice, "Yes?"

"We want to ask you if you would let us into the

tower one more time," Paul said timidly. "We would —."

"Please come back later. I'm working and have no time now."

The children looked at each other in amazement. Now they were certain that more than one person lived in the castle.

They hurried out of the house and back to their own living room, and sat down and stared into the fire in the fireplace.

After a while, Anne shook her head and said, "Something's funny. Professor Crippen interrupted Paul before he could finish his sentence."

"At least one more person must be hiding in the castle," Katie suggested. "Maybe even more. But why? What are they doing there?"

"Who knows if the professor is really an art historian?" Rebecca joined in. "Maybe he belongs to some gang."

"A gang?" Eric asked.

"Yes," insisted Rebecca. "I mean forgers or something."

"Very funny," said Paul. "You've been reading too many adventure books!"

"Well then, what were those sounds you heard?" Rebecca asked, "and what about the person who was in the Knights' Hall?"

"We can find out two things," Anne said. "First, is the professor really researching the history of the castle? We can test him, and we can keep watch in the Knight's Hall to see if he enters and where he disappears to."

"It's simple," she continued. "Frau Martin said

that a history of the castle already exists. We'll read that, or even better, we'll memorize it, and then ask the doctor to explain a few things, just to test his knowledge."

"Not bad!" Paul smiled approvingly. "You've learned quite a lot from me — but I guess you didn't want to tell us your second idea on purpose. Or is it just as simple?"

"What would you do without your big sister?" Anne teased. "Somehow we have to find a way of observing the Knights' Hall."

"Somehow is right—and all our problems will be solved!" Paul exclaimed.

"What's wrong with you two?" Katie looked reproachfully from one to the other. "This arguing won't help us."

"Okay, okay!" Paul stood up. "Do you have a better idea?"

"Maybe we should pray together," Rebecca suggested. The rest of the children sensed that she was right. They all joined hands in a circle and asked God for help.

After the prayer Anne said, "I don't know if we can ask God to help us when we might be doing something wrong."

"We asked God to be with us," Katie replied. "We'll just have to see how everything works out."

"That sounds simple," Paul said. "But how do we know the difference between what we want and what God wants?"

"We could ask Mom," Eric suggested.

"That's the best idea yet," Katie said, smiling at her younger brother.

A short while later Mrs. Baker returned from having taken Tawny for a walk. The moment she entered the living room, she sensed the tense atmosphere. "Well, you all seem to have had an interesting afternoon," she said.

"What do you mean?" asked Anne, trying to sound nonchalant.

"You disappeared for hours and didn't even take Tawny along. Perhaps she'd have been a nuisance to you where you were."

Eric could no longer keep quiet. "We were in the castle."

Then there was no holding the children back. Each one wanted to tell her about the exciting afternoon. After they told her everything, the children were surprised at how calm she was. "While I was in town," Mrs. Baker said, "I met Frau Martin, who told me that she has the key to the castle, and vacationers can go in and out as they wish. Only a few rooms that contain valuable objects, including the library are locked. I was going to tell you about this later. But tell me, how much time passed from the moment you left the Knights' Hall until you heard Professor Crippen's voice at the door?"

"About ten minutes," Rebecca estimated. The others nodded in agreement.

"I would guess that it takes less than a minute to reach Professor Crippen's apartment from the Knights' Hall. I don't see any reason to believe that anyone else is living in the castle. I think you are just prejudiced against the professor."

"He acted strange the very first evening," Anne said, trying to justify her suspicions.

"But what's unusual about that?" Mrs. Baker insisted. "I believe that in 90 percent of all cases, our first impressions are incomplete or incorrect. Many people are shy or reserved around strangers. Some try hard to make a good impression. I don't form an opinion about a person until I really get to know him. Then I try to take him for what he is."

"All right," Anne agreed. "Let's try to find out what Professor Crippen is really like first, and then form our opinion."

"Try to understand," Mrs. Baker continued. "I just want to prevent hasty judgments. We know that Jesus wants us to love everyone. But what is it you want to find out?"

Katie explained, "We want to learn the history of the castle, and then test Professor Crippen's knowledge."

"I don't see anything wrong with that," Mrs. Baker said. "The thing I don't understand is how someone can leave a room without using the door. That is strange."

"We think so too," said Rebecca.

"Tomorrow we're going to find some answers!" Paul exclaimed.

How Many People Live in the Castle?

T he next morning Paul said to the other children, "I have an idea. We could use our intercom to find out when the mystery person enters and leaves the Knights' Hall." The Bakers had brought their intercom system with them. By using its several speakers, they could communicate from any part of the house where there was an electrical outlet.

"That's a great idea!" Katie exclaimed.

The children divided themselves into two groups. Paul and Rebecca were to set up the intercom speakers and listen in on them. The other three wanted to find the history of the castle.

In the Knights' Hall, behind a curtain, Paul found an electrical outlet. He hid the speaker there, and when he tested it, found it broadcast very clearly. Rebecca pressed the buzzer, and Mrs. Baker answered it.

"Now we'll catch the mystery man for sure," Rebecca said.

Back in their apartment, she turned up the intercom speaker as loud as possible and sat down to read a book in one of the comfortable chairs.

The three other children were less successful at first. Frau Martin, who had told them about the castle history, was not at home.

"Maybe we can buy it at a book store," Katie suggested. But this attempt also failed. The clerk did give them the address of the author. He was a retired teacher living on the outskirts of town. Katie, who was slightly disappointed about their results, suggested, "We should pray. God can help us find that book soon."

"Good," Anne said. "We can tell by the way He answers if we're doing the right thing." The three sat down on a bench and prayed.

They approached the author's home and rang the bell. A friendly gray-haired man greeted them. After the children had explained their purpose in coming, he said, "Yes, I wrote that booklet more than thirty years ago. I'll be glad to lend it to you. Please return it to me, because there are only a few copies left. Then if you have any questions, I will try to answer them. By the way, you are fortunate to have found me at home. Normally I would have already gone to do my shopping."

The children were overjoyed. They knew why everything had turned out this way!

Anne descended the front steps, turned and said to the author, "God bless you!"

Surprised, he answered, "Oh, thank you! God bless you too!"

The three ran almost all the way home. They learned from Paul and Rebecca that nothing had happened while they were gone. Except for the steady buzzing, the speaker made no unusual sounds.

"If the mystery man goes through the Knights' Hall this evening or maybe even during the night, we'll never hear it," Eric pointed out.

"Then we'll just keep watch all night," Paul said. "Whoever's on duty can tape the sounds with the cassette recorder. We can take turns. I'm sure Mom will allow that. Anyone who's tired in the morning can sleep in longer."

That evening no one could fall asleep. The children were all wondering what would happen during the night.

It was almost one o'clock, when Katie, trying to appear calm, entered the room where the other children had gathered.

"Why aren't you at your post?" Rebecca asked, frowning.

"Because it's not necessary anymore. The stranger is back in Professor Crippen's room. You can look for yourself. The lights are on over there."

"And what did you hear?" Anne asked.

"Nothing in particular," Katie replied. Yawning, she added, "Listen to the cassette yourselves."

"Okay, let's do it," exclaimed Paul.

In all the excitement, Katie had forgotten to record the first few minutes, so all they heard were the footsteps. They turned off the cassette player.

"Well, that's it for now," said Rebecca. "Let's go to sleep. We'll see what we can find out tomorrow."

Professor Crippen's Secret

T he next morning the children slept in. Then the family met for Bible reading and prayer. While they were eating breakfast, Katie realized that no one was listening to the intercom. Remembering that their experience in the Knights' Hall had taken place around noon, the children all gathered near the speaker in the living room at eleven o'clock. While they waited, they played a game at the table.

Suddenly Eric jumped up and ran to the intercom. Everyone raced to join him. They could clearly hear a door being locked. Twelve footsteps—then a pause. Five more footsteps—then silence.

"Is that all?" murmured Anne, disappointed.

"The last step sounded different," Katie observed. Rebecca and Eric agreed.

"As if it came from a different room," continued Katie. "It echoed slightly." Suddenly she jumped up. "I've got it!" she exclaimed. "There must be a hidden door in that room with a secret passageway on the other side. The moment that person stepped into the passageway, his footsteps echoed. Then the door was closed, and we couldn't hear any more sounds."

"Good thinking!" said Paul.

"Oh, this is exciting!" Rebecca exclaimed. "If we only knew who this person is!"

"We can find out." Paul stood up. "At least we can check to see if it was Professor Crippen's footsteps we heard."

"You mean, we should go to his apartment and see if he's home?" Rebecca asked.

Paul nodded.

The children hurried to the professor's door. Anne lifted the knocker and let it fall. For a few seconds nothing happened.

"Yes?" came the professor's voice from behind the door.

The children stood staring at the door.

Anne interrupted the silence. "What should I say?" she stammered.

"The same thing as yesterday," Katie suggested.

"What was that?"

"Ask if we can climb up the tower again."

Just as Anne uttered her first words, she was cut short. From inside the room came the words, "Please come back later. I'm working and have no time now."

As soon as they were back in the yard, Anne said, "I don't know if it means anything, but the professor's voice sounded strange, as if he had a cold."

"In the middle of the summer?" Eric said.

As the children reached their house, Mrs. Baker came out and asked them to walk the dog.

Rebecca offered to spend some of her allowance on ice cream for everybody. Nobody wanted to miss that, but the children drew straws to decide who would

Tip: On the map, you will find Professor Crippen's apartment on Area Number 1.

stay home at the intercom. Unfortunately for her, Anne lost.

She sat quietly by the intercom. For a half hour nothing happened. Suddenly, through the speaker, she heard something. Quickly she turned on the recorder and continued listening. This time, everything happened in reverse order: five steps, a short pause, then twelve steps. A door was locked. Silence.

Anne sat a while longer in her chair, thinking. An idea had occurred to her, something she very definitely wanted to try.

She left the house, crossed over the yard, and opened the door to the hallway in front of Professor Crippen's door. She had just barely used the knocker when she heard his voice, "Come in."

She heard footsteps approaching. The door handle was pushed down, the key turned, and the door opened.

"Oh, it's you," Professor Crippen greeted her. "What can I do for you?"

"We're wondering if we could go up to the tower again."

"Yes, of course, Tomorrow afternoon would be a good time."

Anne suddenly got the idea she should try to go into the professor's room. "Oh, Professor Crippen. Could we see that booklet on the history of the castle?"

"Yes, I could lend you my copy. One moment please." He disappeared into the room.

Now or never, Anne thought, and followed him. On the table she saw one coffee cup, one plate and some food. She saw nothing suspicious anywhere. When the professor handed her the booklet, she noticed that his right hand was covered with a layer of dust. There was also dust on his pants and shirt.

After thanking the professor, she left and ran toward the village. She found her brothers and sisters in the ice cream shop. Joining them, she sat eating her ice cream and telling them what had happened.

"The table was set for only one person?" Katie inquired.

"Yes."

"If Professor Crippen had dust on his clothes, he could have been in the secret passage," Rebecca suggested. "But then who was in his room when we knocked?"

No one knew the answer. Paul looked at Anne, noting that her brow was wrinkled in thought. "I think you've got some idea."

She shrugged her shoulders. "I don't know, maybe I'm just imagining things."

"Come on, tell us the rest," Eric wriggled in his chair.

"I'm thinking of his voice," Anne said. "At first it sounded as if he had a cold, just like the times we stood at the door. But then when he opened the door, it was different — like normal."

"I don't get it," said Paul. "Come on, let's go back."

On the way home they met Frau Martin. She said, "Tomorrow is Youth Bible Club at our church. You are all welcome to join us."

The children told her they would be happy to come. They started walking back home when Paul moaned, "We can't go to the Bible class! We were going to tour the castle again tomorrow."

"We'll just ask the professor if he has time in the morning," Anne said. "He probably doesn't have any regular schedule for his work."

The children all agreed and continued their walk.

Back in the castle, they decided to talk to Professor Crippen. They entered the hallway. This time it was Rebecca who reached for the door knocker and let it fall against the door. The children waited until they heard Professor Crippen's voice from inside the room. "Yes?"

Rebecca spoke. "Professor Crippen, may we speak to you for a moment because—."

The voice interrupted. "Please come back later. I'm working and have no time now."

"But Professor Crippen, it's important because, we —."

And then it happened! While speaking, Rebecca lifted the knocker and it accidentally fell through her fingers and thudded onto the door again.

"Yes?" the voice repeated.

Rebecca shrugged her shoulders and whispered, "If he's so busy, why does he say yes?"

"Professor, we wanted to say —," Rebecca began.

Again she was cut short, "Please come back later. I'm working and have no time now."

"He keeps repeating himself," Rebecca rolled her eyes.

"That's it!" Paul exclaimed. "Don't you see? He really does repeat himself. He keeps saying the same sentence."

Eric stated what everyone was thinking, "There's

something funny going on here!"

Paul said, "Rebecca, knock on the door again!"

"Not me," she said, backing up. "Do it yourself!"

Paul took hold of the knocker and let it fall against the door. The children heard the usual "Yes?" Katie started to say something, but Paul motioned her to be quiet. They all waited and listened.

Again they heard Professor Crippen's voice. "Please come back later. I'm working and have no time now."

With a mysterious smile, Paul lifted the knob and dropped it. The same words were repeated. After doing this several times, Paul whispered, "Let's go. I'll explain everything outside."

Back in the yard the other children gathered around Paul.

"What you heard wasn't the professor," Paul explained, "only his voice. He seems to have recorded these words on a tape loop."

"Tape loop?" Eric asked.

"Yes. A short tape," Paul explained, "with the ends glued together so that the tape can keep running and repeating the same sentences."

"Who turned on the tape?" Katie wanted to know.

"I think there's a special switch that's triggered by the door knocker."

"But who turned off the tape?" Anne asked.

"It might be a time relay. It runs a few seconds, according to how long it's been set, and then stops. Maybe there's a switch contact on the tape that keeps turning off the recorder at the same place."

"Now I know why his voice sounded as if he had

a cold," Anne explained. "It came out of a loudspeaker."

"I feel better about one thing," Rebecca said. "We have only one person to worry about — the professor."

The others nodded. They decided to return later and ask the professor if he would let them into the tower the next morning.

That evening Mrs. Baker and the children sat around the fireplace and sang. They passed the guitar around so each person could accompany his favorite song.

Mrs. Baker sensed that the children were preoccupied with the mystery and all the unanswered questions. "Let's sing my favorite song," she suggested. The family joined hands and sang together:

My Lord knows the way thru the wilderness—

All I have to do is follow;

Strength for the day is mine all the way,

And all I need for tomorrow;

My Lord knows the way thru the wilderness—

All I have to do is follow.

Good News

As he had agreed, Professor Crippen met the children the next morning to give them another tour of the castle. The children were ready with some questions.

"Will we get to see the wine cellar?" Paul asked. "I bet there are still a few big old barrels there."

The professor grinned, shaking his head. "Castles cannot be compared with normal houses. Usually buildings of this type have no cellar, because they were built on bare rocks. It would have taken too much work to carve out any cellar rooms. So the cellar or kitchen rooms were on the main floor."

"And the dungeons?" Katie asked.

"The dungeons were also on the main floor, usually in the bottom part of the tower."

During the tour, Rebecca pushed down all the door handles and found that several doors were locked.

Noticing this, the professor explained, "Only the baron has keys to those rooms."

Rebecca did not give up, and, having tried another locked door, she asked what was on the other side.

"The library," murmured the professor, continuing on down the hall.

"Oh, we'd like to see that. I'll bet it's full of old books," Paul said. "Do you have the key?"

At first Professor Crippen seemed willing to show them the library, but then he hestitated. "I have a lot of documents and papers spread out in there. I'd have to put them in order first."

Reluctantly he removed the key from his pocket, unlocked the door, opened it a crack, entered quickly, and locked it again. Soon he reopened the door and let the children in. They walked around, fascinated with everything.

"It looks like Dad's study back home." Eric said. "The walls there are full of books too."

They all examined the bookshelves, the large desk, and several old handwritten volumes.

Anne stepped to the window and looked out into the courtyard. *This was the window I saw lit up at night*, she thought. She turned back into the room. *I wonder why there are no papers or documents around. Why did the professor go into the room alone at first? What was he trying to hide?*

"Come along now," the professor urged. Their tour ended on top of the tower. Paul looked out at the castle grounds, trying to fix the location of the various buildings in his mind.

Later at lunch everyone was quiet. All were disappointed that the professor had been so well-informed and had not confirmed their suspicions. During the time that was left before the children would to to Bible Club, they talked about how they might get into the secret passage.

Paul suggested, "We could set up a television camera and record everything on video tape."

"Oh great!" Anne replied. "And where are you going to find a television camera?"

"Do you have a better idea?"

"One of us could hide in the Knights' Hall and watch the professor," Anne suggested.

"From where?" Paul asked. "I don't see any possibilities. The curtains hang very close to the wall, and other than that —"

"I sat under the table, and the professor didn't see me," Eric said proudly.

"He didn't see you," said Katie, "but you couldn't see anything either."

"Don't forget that we were scared and in a hurry," Anne said. "Now we know more and know what to watch for. But who's brave enough to do it?" She looked at Eric.

"There's lots of room under the table," Eric said timidly. "Any one of you could hide there."

"All right, I'll do it," Katie said in a definite voice. "I'll hide and find out where the secret passage is."

The others looked at her with a new respect.

"Okay," Paul said. "And we'll stay as close to the Knights' Hall as we can without being seen. Let's do it right away in the morning."

The children took two guitars and several song books and left for the Bible Club. At the church they found the door locked. But soon Frau Martin appeared with her boys Andreas and Markus and with the key. After several other young people arrived, they all began singing.

Although the Baker children had some difficulty singing the songs in German, many of the tunes were familiar, and they began to feel at home. Paul played guitar for one of the songs.

Markus asked, "Would you teach me how to play like that?"

Frau Martin said, "Why don't you come home with us? You boys could practice together for a while."

At the house Frau Martin served soft drinks, which were refreshing after the hot day.

"How do you like living in the castle?" Andreas inquired.

The Baker children looked at one another, not wanting to betray any of their secrets.

Finally Rebecca blurted out, "Oh, it's very interesting."

Noticing their secretiveness, Markus said, "I suppose you're tracking down the missing treasure?"

"Treasure?" The five Bakers uttered the word almost simultaneously.

"Yes," Markus went on. "A large treasure has been lying hidden in the castle for a long time. According to the legend, anyone who searches for it will pay with his life."

The Bakers stared at Markus in fear.

Suddenly Andreas' laughter brought them back to reality. "Markus is good at telling horror stories. Our younger brother never goes to sleep without looking under his bed!"

"Oh, then Markus' story isn't true," Katie said.

"It's just that he tells stories so realistically—like in a detective movie. But our father says that reality is much less exciting than it appears in the movies."

"How does he know that?" Paul asked.

"Well, he's a police inspector," Andreas

answered proudly.

The Baker children exchanged uneasy glances.

Markus went on with his story. "The legend of the treasure had been passed on from generation to generation."

Frau Martin reentered the room. "As a child I remember a book with stories and legends. The story of the treasure was in that book."

"Do you think we could borrow the book from someone?" Katie asked.

Frau Martin shrugged her shoulders. "Perhaps in our public library. But, now I'm going to get you something cold."

Everyone was pleased with the ice cream she brought. But after the first spoonful, Rebecca could not contain herself. "Why would someone have to pay with his life for searching for the treasure?"

"We don't know why," Andreas replied. "We've heard that a few years ago a man took the story seriously and started hunting for the treasure. One day he disappeared without a trace."

"Maybe he just left," Eric suggested.

"Maybe," Andreas replied. "But it was strange that he left all his belongings behind."

Everyone ate the rest of their ice cream in silence.

"Paul, you're a good guitarist," Andreas said, changing the subject. "I'd like to learn from you."

Paul felt flattered and promised to visit the family the next day. Outside it suddenly turned dark. Heavy clouds hung over the horizon, and Frau Martin advised the children to get home before it started to rain.

They had hardly reached the apartment when the first drops began to fall. A short while later rain streamed onto the roof, and flashes of lightning illuminated the courtyard, making everything look sinister.

Eric remained at the window.

Katie joined him. "Well, what do you see out there?"

"I'm not sure," he replied uncertainly.

"What do you mean?"

"I thought I saw a light down there on the wall."

"A light?"

"Yes. Very dim and just for a second."

"On the wall?"

"Yes, or in the wall."

"In the wall?" Katie looked at him in amazement.

"Maybe it was the moon peeking through the clouds for a moment," Eric said.

Katie had just turned to leave, when Eric called, "Look there! The professor's lights went on."

The lights were burning in the room across the way. Katie shrugged her shoulders. "Oh well, maybe the storm woke him up." She went to where the others were sitting.

"What woke him up?" Eric murmured. "The storm has already moved on." He felt too tired to think, so he walked over to join the others and almost fell asleep during the evening devotions. In his dreams he could still hear the others talking about their plans for the next morning in the Knights' Hall.

Tough Luck

The next morning the children were all excited, wondering if they would solve the mystery of the hidden passageway. Katie seemed more pale than usual. She touched very little of her breakfast.

Mrs. Baker sensed the excitement and asked about their plans for the day.

"Well," Anne replied evasively, "maybe we'll know more in a few hours. You can ask us again at lunch."

Even Tawny seemed to feel the tensions. She paced up and down in the room.

After all had cleared the table, washed dishes, and cleaned the kitchen, Mrs. Baker announced, "I'm taking Tawny for a walk, and then I'm going shopping in the village. Does anyone want to go along?"

She was answered by uneasy silence.

After their mother's departure, the five Bakers reviewed their plans. Rebecca was to stay at home and listen to the intercom speaker.

"If it should get dangerous for Katie," Anne said, "you'll have to notify Mom, or—if she's not home—call Herr Martin."

"Stop talking like that," Katie sighed, "or I won't go through with it! I already have a funny feeling in my stomach."

"Nothing can go wrong," Anne said, trying to reassure her. "Rebecca will be keeping in touch with you. Besides, we'll all be close by."

It was decided that Eric would keep watch from the attic, while Anne and Paul hid in the room next to the Knights' Hall.

At ten o'clock the children started out, expecting the professor around eleven. They quickly reached the Knights' Hall. Eric took his place in the attic. Paul hid behind the door so he could hear the professor approaching. Katie tried out her hiding place inside the table. Anne sat on the rug next to her.

"Ow! I wish I had brought along blankets or pillows. These boards are hard!" Katie complained. Her shoes thumped against the wood.

"You better take those shoes off," Anne said.

Just before eleven o'clock, Paul whispered, "Now."

After the wood had become too hard for her, Katie had climbed out onto the rug. Both girls jumped up. Anne raced toward the next room, and Katie climbed into the table. In all the hurry she slid down too far inside, which she did not notice until she heard the footsteps and discovered that she could not see anything from this position. She racked her brain, trying to think of a way to look out. But the hollow space under the table would echo any movement. She had no choice but to put her head carefully down and wait and listen.

After the steps had faded away, a few minutes passed until she heard a soft "Psst." Paul approached the table and pulled back a chair so his sister could get out. Katie grabbed her shoes and, with Paul and

Anne, slipped out of the Knights' Hall. They picked up Eric in the attic and returned to their apartment.

In the living room, they flopped into their chairs. Everyone waited for Katie's report.

"Come on, tell us what you saw!" Paul urged. Anne perceived the disappointment in Katie's face. "Don't tell us you didn't see anything?"

Katie shook her head.

Paul moaned, "All that effort for nothing! But why?"

Katie explained, and Rebecca comforted her, "That could have happened to me, too, in all that confusion."

Anne thought a moment and then asked, "Should we try it again?"

"If only there was another place to hide," Eric said.

Suddenly Rebecca jumped up from her chair. "What about the two suits of armor by the fireplace? Somebody could hide in one of them."

"I'll do it," declared Paul. "I'll get into one of the suits of armor tomorrow and see everything."

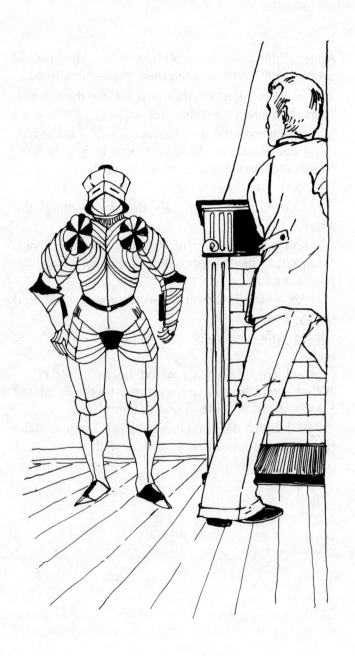

A Place to Hide

That night Paul slept restlessly. All the children were awake earlier than usual. After breakfast the girls wrote postcards to friends and relatives back in the United States. The boys took a stroll with the dog, examining the castle walls from every side. They planned to return exactly at ten o'clock. When they returned, the girls were waiting impatiently.

Soon they reached the Knights' Hall by way of the attic. Quickly they began to take the suit of armor apart.

"Why is the armor so small?" Rebecca asked.

"People were smaller in the Middle Ages," Paul said. "It should fit me just about right."

Paul climbed into the tin leggings and slipped into the chest armor. His sisters fastened the two arm pieces for him and buckled the straps connecting them to the chest piece. The lower part of his body was protected at the front by two loosely hanging metal plates. Paul then donned the helmet and took the sword in his hand. He stepped into place on the stand.

"That looks perfect!" Eric cried.

Everyone waited tensely to see what would happen.

Shortly after eleven o'clock Anne, who had been listening by the door, gave a warning signal. Instantly the four children slipped into the other room.

They had hardly closed the door when Paul gasped. He had forgotten to close the visor on his helmet! He tried to lift his hand, but the armor was too stiff. The footsteps were resounding on the stone stairway. Cold sweat ran down Paul's forehead. Desperately he pressed his head against the helmet and, to his surprise, the visor fell with a loud thud.

Paul trembled in apprehension. Had the professor heard him? It seemed as if he had, because he had hesitated upon entering the room. Now there was silence. *He seems to be looking around*, Paul thought. He felt the cold sweat running down his back. He tried to look out of the slits in the helmet, but it had slipped down, and all he could see was a small part of the floor, not the other side of the room, as he had hoped. Tears of disappointment welled up in his eyes. Then he held his breath! The professor seemed to be taking another route. His steps approached the window. *Will he find the intercom?* Paul wondered. But the footsteps continued around the room.

Slowly they approached the fireplace. Had Professor Crippen noticed something? Paul felt his pulse beating in his temples. Why was nobody at home listening through the intercom? Here they all sat, in a trap! Now the man walked slowly past the armor. Paul caught a glimpse of him. It was definitely the professor! Slowly he walked away only to return again. Through his right slit Paul could see the professor crouch down and look under the table.

Just as he stood up, a crow, taking off from the window ledge, thumped her wings against the window pane. This sound scared the professor, who spun around to look for its source. Relieved, he gave a soft chuckle.

He advanced to the panelled wall. A few seconds later every thing was quiet. After ten minutes of waiting, Paul left his position and walked clumsily toward the next room.

"Oh, you're safe!" Rebecca exclaimed.

Quickly the armor was removed and put back together next to the fireplace. Meanwhile, Anne pressed her ear to the panelling at the point where they thought the secret door might be.

The armor had just been set up when Anne whispered, "Come over here! I keep hearing something, and I don't know where it's coming from."

The others hurried to the panel and listened. They could hear a dull pounding that sounded far away.

"What can that be?" Rebecca looked questioningly at Katie.

"Come on, we'd better go," Anne urged. "Lunch will be waiting for us."

In the courtyard, Anne turned to Paul. "We could tell by the expression on your face that you weren't successful. How did that happen?"

Paul, somewhat crushed, told them his story.

That afternoon the children had to clean their rooms. Paul quickly finished his, then took his guitar and went to visit the Martins.

At first, the others dragged through their chores, but after Rebecca got them all singing, the work was more fun.

As Anne put the broom in the corner, Rebecca called, "Hey Anne, you call that done? The layer of dust on the floor is still so thick a person can see footprints in it." Suddenly she stopped short and sat down on the edge of the bed.

"Is something wrong?" Anne asked.

"No, but I'm wondering if we can outwit the professor with footprints."

"With footprints?"

"Listen," she explained. "If we take a piece of cloth and fill it with sand from the courtyard and then remove the sand carefully without shaking the cloth —"

"And then what?"

"Well, then we'd shake out the cloth in front of the panelling, which would create a very thin layer of dust, unnoticeable to the professor. By studying this dust layer after he disappeared behind the wall, we could find the location of the secret door."

"Good thinking!" Anne declared.

"If one of us set this trap before we go to church tomorrow, we'd get somewhere in our search."

"How are you coming?" Katie entered with Eric. The two girls told them of the new plan. Hopes grew. Maybe now they'd be able to unlock the secret.

When Paul returned from the Martins, he had much to tell. During his visit, he had met Herr Martin. His picture of a tough police inspector had been completely changed. Herr Martin was a quiet, friendly man, and a born-again Christian.

View from the Mountain

T he next morning was Sunday, and the sun shone brightly into the dining room. The family took their time at breakfast. They had lots of time until the ten o'clock church service. They had arrived a whole week ago, but the days had flown by!

When they arrived at the church, they found that because the pastor was on vacation, Herr Martin would conduct the service. He asked Mrs. Baker to serve as organist. The Baker children did their best in following along in the German service.

Back in the apartment after church Katie and Rebecca made pizzas for lunch. Later the children started hiking to the mountainside overlooking the castle.

On the way up, Anne groaned, "I thought we were going for a walk, not running a race!"

At a pleasant spot above the castle, they rested and gazed at the castle spread out below them.

"The castle sure looks different from up here!" Eric exclaimed.

"Look," Katie pointed toward the castle. "There's the window we crawled through. As far as I can tell, we have never been in the left section, in the little towers and on the castle wall."

"I thought we had seen everything," Anne said.

"No, I don't think so," Katie replied.

"Can you really tell where we were on the tour with all those stairs, corridors, and rooms?" Anne asked.

As well as she could, Katie drew a map of the castle in the dirt. She explained, "We climbed in here. Over here is the Knights' Hall. About here is the professor's room. There's the tower, and here's the library." Katie pointed to a narrow building. "We were never in that part."

Mrs. Baker joined them and asked, "What are you doing?"

Rebecca showed her the sketch. "Katie is sure that we haven't been in this part of the castle."

Mrs. Baker shrugged her shoulders. "It's possible. Perhaps those are the rooms in which the baron lives when he visits the castle."

Katie shook her head, "No, I don't think so."

After a picnic supper, the family started down. The path led them into the valley, along a stream, past several waterfalls to the lake shore. They stopped at the old mill. "I'd like to take a good look at that some day," Paul said.

"It looks so mysterious," Anne added, trying to look through a dusty window.

"Look," Eric pointed up the mountain. "We can see the castle from here. It looks like the part we haven't seen. If those are the baron's windows, he has a great view of the lake and the mill."

"I'd like to see more of the area," Paul said. "Could we take a ride in the van for an hour or so?"

Mrs. Baker nodded. "Sure, if that's what you all want to do." An hour lengthened to three. All the

Bakers were fascinated by the beauty of the region.

On the drive back, they approached a wide valley. Everyone looked up in amazement. Before them stood the castle, brilliantly lit up by a spotlight. "Look at that," Eric exclaimed. "It looks like the castle is floating in the air."

Because the night was very dark, the horizon was invisible. The castle seemed to glow in a supernatural way.

"It reminds me of the new Jerusalem in the Bible," Rebecca declared.

"What do you mean?" Eric asked.

"Paul, why don't you read it from the Bible," Mrs. Baker suggested. "It's in Revelation 21."

Paul took the Bible from the glove compartment and found the chapter. Everyone listened closely as he read.

Then I saw a new earth (with no oceans!) and a new sky, for the present earth and sky had disappeared.

And I, John, saw the Holy City, the new Jerusalem, coming down from God out of heaven. It was a glorious sight, beautiful as a bride at her wedding.

I heard a loud shout from the throne saying, "Look, the home of God is now among men, and He will live with them and they will be His people; yes, God Himself will be among them.

"He will wipe away all tears from their eyes, and there shall be no more death, nor sorrow, nor crying, nor pain. All of that has gone forever."

And the one sitting on the throne said, "See, I am making all things new!" And then He said to me,

"Write this down, for what I tell you is trustworthy and true" (Revelation 21:1-5, The Living Bible).

"Wow!" said Katie. "It sounds as if the new Jerusalem will be even more beautiful and better than our castle."

Where Is the Treasure?

The next morning Paul planned to shake out the dusty cloth in the Knights' Hall. Eric was to stay at the intercom. Katie and Anne wanted to visit the village library to learn more about the legend of the treasure. Mrs. Baker sent Rebecca to the village to buy a new can opener.

The three girls left for town together. Anne and Katie arrived at the library to discover that it would not be open until eleven o'clock.

"We'll have to wait another hour," Katie murmured. The two girls decided to spend the time looking in the windows of the little shops.

Meanwhile Rebecca had found a hardware store. Near the door were racks of kitchen utensils. She began searching for a can opener. Suddenly she stopped. From another part of the store she heard a familiar voice. It was Professor Crippen!

The saleswoman seemed to be explaining something. "I'd suggest that you take the big cartridges, so that you won't have to buy them every week."

While the professor was leaving, Rebecca hid behind some high shelves. *If only I could find out what he bought*, she thought. *If I dare ask the saleswoman, she might get suspicious.* Rebecca folded her hands and prayed, "Dear Lord Jesus, give me courage!" Then she took a can opener from the rack and stepped to the cash register.

"Oh, you've already helped yourself," the clerk scolded. "In the future please come to me first. I don't like it when children get things mixed up."

"I didn't get anything mixed up. I just took this can opener off the rack."

"Yes, that's what they all say, and then I have to put everything back in place."

Now what should I do? Rebecca wondered. *Katie would probably leave the store immediately and buy the can opener somewhere else. But I'm afraid to try that,* she thought. Besides, she was still curious about the cartridges the professor had bought. She knew they weren't gun cartridges, because she had seen some when her father had gone hunting back in America. These cartridges on the counter were thicker and painted blue.

She was about to pay for the can opener and leave the store, when she remembered her prayer for courage. "Excuse me. The man who just left bought some large cartridges. Could I ask what they're used for? They're not for a gun are they?"

Rebecca's friendly words melted the reserve of the clerk. The woman chuckled. "Those cartridges are too big for a gun, except maybe a cannon. They're gas cartridges used for camping, in stoves, and for lamps. A few weeks ago Professor Crippen bought a gas lamp that uses cartridges like these."

"Why does he need that?" Rebecca inquired. "There's electricity in the castle."

The clerk shrugged her shoulders. Rebecca could tell she really wasn't interested. "Perhaps he uses it someplace where there are no electric lights. Well, now I have to get back to my work."

Rebecca paid for the can opener, thanked the woman, and left the store, pleased with what she had learned.

At home Rebecca waited impatiently for Katie and Anne. When the girls finally returned, they had some news to report.

"The library has the book about the castle, but it's checked out," Anne said. She looked puzzled. "But we don't know who has it."

"What about the professor?" Rebecca suggested.

"Could be," Anne agreed.

"The librarian told us that the book is overdue," Katie said. "Because no one has asked for it, she hasn't called for the book. Maybe we could go and ask the professor if he has it."

"Okay, let's go," Rebecca replied.

At first the professor seemed surprised, then he gave them the book, saying, "There are some very nice stories in it. One of them is about this castle. It even tells about a treasure. But, of course, there are lots of stories like that about castles."

The girls thanked him for the book and returned to their apartment. Anne offered to read the book in the afternoon and tell the others about it in the evening.

"Where are the boys?" Katie asked.

"Eric is sitting by the intercom," their mother reported. "Paul said he had some exploring to do."

After he had spread a thin layer of dust along the wall in the Knights' Hall, Paul prepared for a long wait. The professor would not be coming until eleven o'clock. Paul kept thinking about the windows Katie and Rebecca had seen from the mountain. With this in mind, he climbed the stairs to the attic. *This attic must connect with the house next door*, he thought. At first he could not find a connecting door, but pushing aside some junk he saw a small opening, a space between the rafters only two feet high. He could look through into another attic, which was lighted by a small window.

Should I crawl through? he wondered. It was dusty, but it might be worth it. Because the attic next door was lighted, anyone approaching could see the opening, so Paul pulled a chest and some other stuff in front of it. Then he crawled behind the chest and wriggled through the opening.

He couldn't open the window, but through the dusty panes he could see far past the village. Across the room he saw a door and tried to open it. It creaked loudly. Paul was sure the noise could be heard all the way to the ground floor. *If only I had some oil to lubricate the hinges*, he thought.

Then he had an idea. *Maybe I could use spit. But I'll still have to pry up the door.*

Paul crawled back to the other attic and searched through the junk for something to use as a tool. He found a broken-off chair leg and another board to use as a fulcrum. He jammed a chair leg under the door and pushed the board underneath. When he stepped on the chair leg, it worked like a lever to lift the door. He "oiled" the hinges with spit, and was able to open the door with hardly a sound.

The door led to a staircase. Paul thought he recognized it as the one that led to the library. Should he take a quick look at the library? Maybe he could see what the professor wanted to hide from them. But where was the professor now? In the secret passage — or even in the library itself? *That wouldn't be too good*, Paul thought.

Cautiously approaching the library, he looked through the keyhole. Many old books, some open, were lying on the table. Should he take a chance and enter? Hesitantly he put his hand on the door handle. Suddenly a clicking sound followed by clattering sent him dashing up the stairs. Then he heard a small bronze gong. A smile crossed his face. An old wall clock had made him run!

Paul decided it was time to check on the Knights' Hall. He entered the room and, kneeling down, found some barely visible footprints. From the door they led to the fifth panel. Paul felt every board and pressed every molding. Nothing moved. About the panelling hung a three-armed candle holder. As much as he tried to move it, to the right and to the left, up or down, nothing happened.

Disappointed, he studied the remaining tracks. They ended three panels farther. The professor must have passed through a hidden opening, but there still was no way to discover it. Only one possibility remained: someone would have to observe the professor entering the secret passageway. Unfortunately, there didn't seem to be any hiding place except the suit of armor.

Back in the apartment he reported to the other children. "I'd like to have a look at those papers in the library," Paul said. "Maybe we could take pictures of them with Mom's pocket camera. It has a special close-up lens."

"But we still have to find out exactly when the

professor comes and goes," Rebecca said.

"I have an idea," Katie offered. "Suppose Paul were in the library and the professor would enter the Knights' Hall earlier than expected. We could hear that on the intercom."

"Okay," Eric replied. "But then how do we warn Paul?"

"Let me finish," Katie said impatiently. "Let's say Eric and Rebecca were at the intercom. Anne and I could wait outside. When they heard the professor coming, they could give us a signal through the window. Then we could yell to Paul."

"That would make too much noise," Paul said. "The professor would hear you."

"That's right. But listen. We often call the dog when she's outside and is supposed to come in. The professor has heard us do that. When Paul hears us call Tawny several times, he'll know that someone is coming."

Paul said, "Okay, let's give it a try tomorrow."

"Where's Anne?" asked Rebecca. "Still reading that book?"

After dinner Anne reported to the others. "Here's what I found out. During the Peasants' Revolt of 1525 the castle was besieged for a short time. The peasants had heard that some nobles had hidden their valuable possessions there. The lord of the castle had always gotten along with the peasants, so he wasn't expecting any trouble.

"The peasants forced the lord to surrender and demanded that he hand over the treasure. Inside the castle walls, the rebels searched and found nothing. They took the lord and his two sons captive. They were never heard from again. The nobles who escaped were captured a short time later. After being tortured, they confessed they had given their belongings to the lord before escaping through a secret passage. It seems that only the lord and his sons knew about the hiding place. When they died, they took the secret with them."

"Did you find out anything else?" Eric asked.

"Well, there was something else, but you won't like it. Some people think that this legend was just made up to confuse the peasants and draw attention to the castle while the nobles escaped with their treasures. Of course, this is just a theory. The castle has been searched many times but neither a secret passage nor a treasure was found." She leaned back and looked at the others.

"Well, we're going to find the treasure!" Katie cried and jumped up.

"What do you mean?" Rebecca asked.

"Well, we know that there is a secret passage, so the other part of the story must be true, too."

"It will either be us or the professor," Paul added.

Now they all knew what Professor Crippen was searching for. He must be working in some unknown part of the castle. That's why he needed so many gas cartridges.

"Do we have the right to stop him?" Paul wondered.

"Of course," Rebecca said. "He's a crook, looking for a treasure while pretending to study the history of the castle."

"No one can prove that," Katie said. "Maybe he just happened to read this legend and wants to find the treasure and turn it over to the baron."

"There's just one thing we can do," Anne suggested. "Continue to search and find out as much as possible. If the professor is an honest person, then everything is all right. If not, then we're working on a genuine criminal case, and we could be in real danger if the professor finds out."

A Secret Visit

T he next morning Paul and Eric waited until they heard the professor's footsteps in the Knights' Hall. Then they made their way to the library. Cautiously Paul took hold of the door handle — and it opened! The table was covered with documents and papers. "Look here," Paul pointed to one book. "This is that book of legends. So there are two copies!" Carefully, the boys picked up the old documents, some of them on thin parchment.

Suddenly Eric cried, "Look what I found!"

Paul examined the parchment closely. It was a map of the castle. Next to it lay a newer copy, probably drawn by the professor with some added details. "Do you see that? A hallway and a cellar have been drawn in with pencil." His hands shook as he lifted the drawing to get a closer look.

"Should we take it with us?" Eric asked.

"No. First of all that would be stealing, and besides the professor would notice. But we could copy it. I brought some paper along."

Paul began copying the map. Eric started photographing the documents and articles. Afterward he pulled several books off of the shelves, hoping to find something of importance.

"Hurry up, Paul, will you? I don't like it here."

Suddenly the boys heard from the courtyard, "Tawny, Tawny."

Paul grabbed the camera and his copy of the map, and both boys raced out of the room and soon were back with the other children.

"What happened?" Paul asked breathlessly.

"Oh, you won't believe it!" Katie said, shaking her head. "Rebecca got bored, so she looked out the window and waved to us. Anne thought she was signalling us to call Tawny."

Rebecca stood looking embarrassed.

Paul said, "Well, forget it. At least I had time to finish this." He showed them the diagram of the castle. "Now we need to get this film developed."

"You know, the professor lied to us when he said there was no cellar," Eric said. "And look, the outer wall is much higher where the cellar seems to be."

"I think it goes deeper, because the top is the same height all over," Paul added.

"Okay. That means the cliff must have been lower on that side, so when they built the castle, it formed a basement there," Anne suggested.

"Well, the professor must spend a lot of time down in that cellar," Katie said. "Is he looking for the treasure? If so, how come it's taking him so long? If he hasn't found it yet, there's still hope for us."

"You make it sound so simple," Anne said, frowning. "We don't know where the secret passage is, and even if we did, the professor is always down there. We don't have a chance."

"If there is a passage into the cellar, it must be visible somewhere," Paul said. "We should take a look at the rooms at the side under the Knights' Hall.

The secret passage has to lead downwards, and some wall must be thicker and one room narrower. I'd like to check on that."

"With our luck the passage might just lead to a dead end," Katie replied gloomily.

"Oh, come on. Let's go look fast, before the professor comes back!" Rebecca urged.

She and Paul accompanied Katie. Below the Knights' Hall they found a kitchen. At first they saw nothing unusual. Katie looked at the fireplace. "The passageway should come out here."

"That's a huge fireplace!" Rebecca said.

"Do you notice anything?" Katie asked. "It's large on the outside but much smaller inside."

"Man, that's really well-camouflaged! Hey, Paul, get a look at this!"

They had discovered some new evidence, but for now it was no help to them .

Paul looked at the floor. "I've found something! It looks like powder. What do you think it is? It's hard to tell here in the dark."

"Let's take a sample with us," Katie suggested.

She pulled a handkerchief out of her pocket and filled it with some of the powder. "We can examine it later."

"Here's something else." Paul pointed to some footprints on the steps.

"Where do they go to? Let's find out," Katie suggested.

"Just so the professor doesn't catch us," Rebecca warned.

Climbing the stairs, Paul said, "Here are more tracks. They lead to the Knights' Hall and end right where we think the secret passage is."

"The professor seems to have carried something downstairs," Rebecca said. "Let's go check out that powder."

Back in the kitchen the three children studied the powder.

"Can you tell what it is, Paul?" Rebecca asked.

"Well, I have an idea. I'm going to add some water to it. Then we'll wait and see."

The Hidden Cellar

As soon as he woke up the next morning Paul examined the powder sample. It was stone hard. *Cement*, he thought. *But what does the professor do with cement?* He discussed this with the others, who were equally puzzled. They agreed that someone hunting for treasure might have to move some stones, but cement was necessary only for building. What could the professor be building?

After breakfast Eric played with the dog, while Rebecca and Katie had fun with a stray kitten they had found. Paul inspected the tiny ferns that grew on the castle wall. While doing this, he discovered a small opening that seemed to go deeper into the wall. *I wonder how far that goes in?* he thought. He began looking for some sort of measuring stick. Finding nothing in the courtyard, he continued his search on the path in front of the castle gate. Finally he found a stick about two feet long. He soon found that the hole was deeper than that. His curiosity growing, he went in search of a longer stick. Outside the castle wall he found a dead branch about six feet long.

When he returned, Katie asked, "What are you going to do with that?"

"I want to measure the depth of a crack."

"Do you need such a long stick?"

"Yes. The crack seems to be very deep."

Katie watched Paul insert the branch into the opening. She was amazed to see the long stick vanish.

"Rebecca, come over here," she called.

"What do you suppose is behind this crack?" Paul asked.

Rebecca tried to look through. "I can't see anything. If we'd take out this stone, we could see more." She pointed to a small stone next to the crack.

"I could do it with a small chisel," Paul said. "Too bad we don't have one."

"Should I get a big screwdriver and a hammer from the van?" Rebecca offered.

Paul nodded. She was able to find the car keys, unlock the van and get the needed tools, lock the van again, and return the keys to their kitchen hook without Mrs. Baker noticing.

"Let me do it," Katie begged. The work was easy, because the mortar between the stones was very sandy.

Meanwhile Rebecca examined the wall. "All the other stones are much larger. This one is different. Maybe it was put in later."

After a few moments the stone was removed. The children gathered around the opening, a shaft about as wide as the stone they had taken out.

"Does the hole go in very deep?" Katie asked. "I'll try yelling into it. Hello!" she called. "Did you hear that?"

Everyone took turns shouting into the hole. All they heard were their own echoes.

"This means the hole is very deep," Paul said, "or there's a room at the end."

He had hardly spoken these words when Katie

and Rebecca simultaneously exclaimed, "The hidden cellar!"

Katie looked at her watch and said, "The professor is coming soon. He usually enters the cellar at eleven o'clock. Maybe he could see daylight from the inside. Let's put the stone back!"

"I have an idea!" Rebecca's face shone with excitement. "Let's find out if it really is the hidden cellar."

"What's your idea?" Katie asked.

"We'll put our ears to the opening and listen. Paul can listen to the intercom so that we don't miss Professor Crippen."

"What kind of a sign should I give you?" Paul asked.

"As soon as you hear something, run to the window and call Tawny. Then we'll know it's time to use our ears."

The girls waited a long time. Finally the awaited warning came. The girls strained their ears and heard footsteps descend the stairs and then fade away. It was the hidden cellar!

After lunch Katie stepped over to the window. Suddenly she turned and asked, "Eric, did you see light over there during that last thunderstorm?"

"Yes, I think it was there."

"You saw light through that narrow slit?" Katie asked dubiously.

"Why not?" Rebecca said. "Gas lamps are very bright, and besides it was pitch dark outside."

That night, after they had said their prayers, Rebecca looked out the window into the darkness. "O Lord, be with us tomorrow," she murmured.

The Mysterious Well

The next day Eric and Rebecca were playing with the kitten, which had now taken up residence in the castle. Tawny was sniffing around the courtyard. Suddenly it seemed as if the dog realized that the kitten was getting all the attention. As soon as the children left the kitten alone and it began smelling a bone the dog had left there, Tawny barked loudly and bounded toward the kitten.

A wild chase began. The kitten made the mistake of fleeing to the enclosed part of the courtyard and found no way to escape. The well, four feet high and covered with sheet metal, seemed to offer the only protection. The two animals ran round and round it.

"Tawny, stop it!" Eric shouted.

In the excitement of the chase, she did not listen.

Suddenly the chase seemed to be at an end. Tawny was sniffing at the edge of the well, and Eric thought the cat had escaped. But several minutes later he noticed the dog return to sniff at the well again. The third time this happened, Eric ran to the edge of the well. Tawny seemed to have a guilty look on her face. Then Alexander heard a pitiful *meow* and saw that the dog was smelling at a certain part of the lid to the well. The cat had hidden in the well and now was unable to get out. Eric ran to tell the others.

Because Katie and Paul were busy playing a

game, Paul said, "Just lock the dog in the house. Then the kitten will come out by herself."

Eric tried that, but for almost an hour he continued to hear the kitten's soft cry. He went to Paul and Katie again.

Paul looked somewhat impatiently at his younger brother. "If nothing else works, we'll have to lift the lid and get the cat out, I suppose."

"Maybe the well is deep and spooky," Katie added.

"Let's have a look at it." Paul jumped up and went to the well.

After a quick examination, he muttered, "The lid is screwed on. How can we open it?"

"I think there's a tire wrench in the van," Eric said. "Would that work?" He ran to fetch the tool.

It fit, but the children were not strong enough to loosen the rusty screws.

Standing there helplessly, Rebecca recalled, "When Dad was changing the snow tires in spring and the bolts were too tight, he used a pipe to make the tire wrench longer. But where could we get something like that?"

"The blacksmith might lend us a pipe," Eric suggested.

"Good idea," Paul agreed. "Let's try it. Come on, let's go!"

The blacksmith lived between the castle and the village. The children arrived there in minutes. The blacksmith was friendly and agreed to lend them a pipe.

When they returned, the soft *meows* were still coming from the well. Using the pipe and pushing together the children were able to loosen the screws. The lid was lighter than the children had imagined and easy to lift. All five children approached the edge of the well. At first they saw only the little cat. It had scrambled up to a small protruding stone, but did not have the courage to jump the rest of the way.

Katie and Paul held onto Anne while she bent down to rescue the kitten. No sooner did she have it than it leaped from her arms and was soon out of sight.

"Poor thing, it must have been scared to death!" Rebecca said.

"Look! There's something like a ladder in the well," Paul said, pointing to holes in the wall at regular intervals.

"What were the holes used for?" Eric asked.

"To climb down on, I guess," Rebecca replied. "The men who built this well had to work a long way down."

Katie picked up a stone and dropped it into the well. It took some time before they heard it hit the bottom.

"I'd like to see what it looks like down there." Paul peered into dark depths. "An adult might be able to climb down if he pushed his back against one side and used his feet for support on the opposite side."

"We need an electric lamp," Rebecca said.

"If we can figure the distance from the house and add the depth of the well to it, we would need an awfully long cord. Where could we get it?" Paul asked.

"The simplest thing would be to buy one of those gas lamps and let it down on a string," Eric suggested.

"Hey, not a bad idea!" Katie exclaimed.

Eagerly Eric continued. "We could pay for it with

our allowance money."

"Now wait a minute!" Anne protested. "That's too much of a sacrifice just for a look into a well."

"All right," Paul said. "I'll pay a double share."

Katie and Paul started out for the village to buy a lamp and string.

An hour later all the children, except Anne, were standing expectantly at the well. Paul lit the lamp and slowly let it down into the well. Even though the light was very bright, it did not shine downwards. So it was a long time before the children could see the bottom.

Katie was disappointed, "Too bad. Just rocks and a few branches— and a rope."

"A rope? Then someone else must have climbed down there," exclaimed Rebecca. "But why? We can see everything from up here."

"With a lamp," Eric added.

"Even a burning newspaper thrown down there would be enough," Rebecca said and slapped her cheek as it occurred to her that this would have been less expensive than the lamp.

Eric said, "I can't imagine what anyone would be looking for down there."

Katie was the first to get up. "Well, what are we going to do now?"

"I was afraid that we wouldn't see anything unusual," Paul said in defeat. "Oh well, it doesn't matter. We may be able to use the lamp some other time. I'll pull it back up, and we can close the lid again."

While Paul was pulling up the lamp, Eric continued looking down the well. Suddenly he jumped up. "Let the lamp back down again."

"Why?" Paul asked.

"Just lower the lamp again!" Eric begged.

Because Eric would not give a reason, Paul stubbornly continued to lift the lamp.

Seeing this, Katie looked at Paul impatiently and said, "Okay, Eric, I'll do it for you."

She took the string out of Paul's hands, and he stomped off.

"Did you see something, Eric?" Katie inquired.

He shrugged his shoulders, "Come over here. I'll show you what I saw."

He took the string in his hand, held it over the middle of the well, and let it swing back and forth.

Before he could explain, Katie gasped, "Hey, the lamp disappears under a ledge. There must be a hollow space underneath it. I wonder how big it is."

"I'll let the string down a little more," Eric said.

"Really! There could be a room or a passageway underneath. Listen, come here everyone! We may have discovered a passageway!"

Paul raced back to the well. Everyone started talking at once.

Finally Rebecca suggested, "One of us has to be let down into the well to take a look."

"Great!" Katie said. "You suggested it, so you can be the one!"

"Well, I just thought that *someone* could have a look," Rebecca murmured.

Eric came to her defense. "It's not going to be easy. Besides, we don't have a rope that's long enough."

"Would a mirror work?" Rebecca asked.

"That's an idea. I'll get one out of our hallway," Katie said, heading for the apartment.

When she returned, she laid a long piece of kite string on the well's edge. "Maybe we'll have some use for that."

First the mirror was tied onto the lamp string. Then the children decided to tie the kite string onto the bottom of the mirror. This way the mirror could be lowered to a certain depth and then tilted with the second string. At a 45-degree angle they would be able to look around the corner. The lamp directly over the mirror provided light. The string was lowered into the depths. With trembling hands, Rebecca tugged gently on the thin second string.

The children held their breath. They glimpsed a dark hole in the side of the well. It was about three feet from the bottom and seemed to be four or five feet high.

Rebecca was the first to find words. "A hidden tunnel!" Her voice trembled. They had seen many things during the twelve days at their adventure castle, but this was a special discovery.

"A secret passage," Eric whispered.

Anne, who had gone to the house for a glass of milk, came to the front door. She saw that the others were still at the well.

The children were so occupied with their thoughts that they did not notice Anne until she stood next to them and asked casually, "What do you see down there?"

Katie, looking at her as if she were from another planet, exclaimed, "We've discovered a secret passage!"

In disbelief Anne looked down the well. "Then it was a good thing you bought the lamp after all," she admitted.

"We'll have to explore the tunnel!" Eric cried, his eyes shining with excitement.

"You're right," Katie said. "But how?"

"We need a ladder, but we don't have one. Besides such a long one would be too heavy," Paul replied.

"A thick rope would be almost as good. We could knot it if we had one," Eric suggested.

"I know what!" Rebecca exclaimed, dancing back and forth.

"Well, what?" Paul asked.

"I'll be right back." She ran across the yard, through the gate, and toward the house.

The other children looked at each other and shrugged their shoulders.

After a few minutes Rebecca returned with a tow-rope rigging in her hand. Father had bought it after their van had gotten stuck on sandy ground. With the rope tied to one end of the van, and the other end fastened with a pulley to a tree, it was possible to pull the van out of sand or mud with very little effort.

"This is what we need!" Triumphantly Rebecca held the rigging.

"Great!" Paul muttered. "Now all we need is a tree trunk that we can put over the top of the opening."

"I saw a big log in back of the house," Eric said. "Maybe it will do. Come one, Paul, help me carry it."

The log was long and strong enough. The boys began to attach the rope and pulley. Some ten feet from the end of the rope, Paul tied a knot through which a hook was hung, creating a loop that could not be tightened. A thick mat was found to make a comfortable seat.

"Who wants to be first?" Paul looked around at everyone.

After some hesitation Rebecca said, "I do, if someone else goes along."

"I'll be second," Paul chimed in.

"And then it's my turn," Katie proclaimed.

"If you go down another time, I'll go along," Eric offered rather timidly.

"Good. I'll stay up here and lower you, and if you behave, I'll lift you out again," Anne said teasingly.

"Well, Rebecca, what are you waiting for?" Paul asked.

"I feel funny."

"Must be fear," Paul quipped.

"That's a big help!" Rebecca looked as if she might cry.

"I'm sorry," Paul stammered. "Maybe we should pray for courage."

Rebecca looked at him with gratitude. The children prayed together and put this adventure and the whole day in God's hands.

An Amazing Discovery

R ebecca crawled into the loop Paul had fixed. "Be careful," Anne said. "It's a long way to the bottom of the well."

With pounding hearts the other children watched Rebecca disappear down the well. Soon they heard her call, "Everything's all right!"

Paul loosened a small lever and was ready to pull the rope up in a few seconds.

"Can you see anything?" Anne stared down into the well. Rebecca had set the lamp into the secret passage. "No," her voice echoed. "There's a bend in the tunnel after about ten feet. I'd rather wait for Paul."

Her older brother had already climbed into the loop and was waiting impatiently for Anne to let him down. Arriving at the bottom of the well, he called up, "We're going to enter the secret passage."

"Don't go too far." Katie began to seat herself in the loop.

Then it happened. A bloodcurdling scream tore the silence.

"That's Rebecca!" Katie cried.

"Oh, she's probably just kidding!" Anne said. "Come on, let me down."

"No, it's for real! She's scared!"

Katie turned pale and climbed out of the loop.

Rebecca was still screaming. The children heard her call, "Pull me out. Quick!"

Anne let down the rope as fast as she could. The loop had scarcely reached the bottom when Rebecca called out, "Quick, pull me up!"

As soon as she was out of the well, Rebecca exclaimed breathlessly, "There's a skeleton down there!"

"A what?" Katie and Anne stared at one another.

Paul's voice interrupted their shock. "Hey, are you going to leave me down here?"

Anne sprang to the well and pulled him up. He too was pale, but less rattled than Rebecca.

"Is it a real skeleton?" Eric asked, his eyes wide.

Paul nodded. "The man is still clothed, but you can see his skull and the bones of his hands."

"What about the passage?" Anne asked.

"I don't know. In all the excitement Rebecca dropped the lamp. Before we came to the skeleton, I thought I could see stones and sand blocking the way about thirty feet farther on, but I'm not sure."

"Could you tell what direction the tunnel goes?" Katie inquired.

Paul pointed toward the main building. "It might go clear to the house, or to the cellar underneath."

"What do we do now?" Anne asked.

"Maybe we should ask Mom," Rebecca suggested.

Everyone agreed that this was a good idea.

After hearing everything Mrs. Baker said firmly, "First we have to inform the police." She went to the telephone and asked to be connected with Herr

Martin. After hanging up, she announced, "Herr Martin will be right here. He's calling the Fire Department. They'll bring a long ladder to reach down the well. The Homicide Squad from Munich will also be alerted."

"Homicide Squad?" Eric exclaimed.

"Yes," Mrs. Baker nodded. "No one knows why this man died or how he got into the well."

Soon a car entered the courtyard. The children dashed outside. Herr Martin greeted them warmly and listened to their story. Both policemen who had accompanied him stood around and waited for the Fire Department.

Soon a truck with two firemen arrived, and parts of a ladder were lowered into the well and screwed together, piece by piece. As soon as this was finished, Herr Martin took a strong flashlight and climbed down into the well. Paul asked him to inspect the whole passageway and to retrieve the gas lamp.

Ten minutes later, having reached the top of the well again, Herr Martin shrugged his shoulders. "It's hard to say. We'll have to leave it up to the experts. Oh yes, the passage. It ends after about thirty feet. It looks as if it had caved in, though the arch is intact. The path is blocked with stones and sand. Someone must have tried to dig the sand away. It was probably that poor fellow down there. The tools are completely rusted." He turned to one of the other policemen. "I'm driving to the office. You stay here until the homicide men have finished their work."

Another three hours passed before the detectives appeared. After hearing the childrens' brief report, they climbed into the well, taking their camera equipment along.

One of the policemen turned to the children. "You may as well go to bed. They won't tell you anything."

The Baker children were disappointed. Then they noticed that it was already nine o'clock, so they went into the house.

When it was finally time to go to bed, they saw that several cars were still parked in the courtyard. They asked if they could go outside again, and their mother gave permission.

At the well they encountered Professor Crippen.

"Well, children, congratulations. That was very clever of you. Tell me more about the tunnel."

Paul started to describe everything, until he noticed the warning expression in Anne's eyes.

The professor seemed to have heard enough. "Thank you very much for that information. I'm sure the passageway was to bring water into the castle. Nothing really special. Good night."

The children saw him turn and disappear into the darkness.

The Skeleton's Story

P aul went out into the courtyard early the next morning. There were no policemen or firemen to be seen. The well was covered again.

At ten o'clock the phone rang, and Mrs. Baker answered. It was the police.

After she hung up, she gathered the children around her and reported on the conversation. "The skeleton had many broken bones. The police also found a frayed rope with a torn loop on the end. The police assume this is the man who was searching for the treasure many years ago and disappeared. He must have lowered himself into the well with the rope without noticing that the iron ring on the edge of the well rim was very sharp. After he had climbed up and down several times, the rope was worn enough, and the man fell, breaking both his legs. In this remote part of the courtyard no one could hear him calling. It looks as if he dragged himself to the edge, but no help came, and he died."

"Oh, the poor man!" Katie exclaimed. "But at least now his relatives will know what happened."

For the rest of the day the children did not feel like looking for any more adventure. They decided, instead, to go to the swimming pool. Eric suggested they invite the Martin boys.

The children had fun swimming and playing in

the water. Later they had a picnic and sat around singing some Christian songs. Some other children were attracted by the singing, and soon the Bakers and the Martins were able to share their faith in God.

Back home in the evening the children thanked the Lord for the afternoon, which had brought not only fun, but an opportunity to witness for Jesus Christ.

Where Is Professor Crippen?

T he next day Eric exclaimed, "Tomorrow Dad is coming!"

"Yea!" Katie cried. "Maybe he'll know of a way to find out the secret of the passageway."

"We still have lots of exploring to do," Rebecca said. "There are so many rooms we haven't seen. I'd like to go to the chapel again too."

"I just don't understand," Anne said. "Why would a spring that starts under a house be piped into a well. It would be much simpler to pump up the water."

"Maybe pumps weren't invented then," Eric surmised. "Maybe the water was supposed to be for everybody. The well is easy to reach from the houses."

Suddenly Rebecca jumped up and ran to get paper and pencil. She drew a sketch of the castle, explaining, "The supposed water tunnel runs in this direction. Judging from the crack in the wall, the passageway must lead right along here." She pointed to the drawing with her pencil. "Do you see what I see?"

Nobody replied.

"Probably both passageways are connected, or were connected," she added. "Remember the sand blocking the way?"

Katie rose from her chair. "We just have to solve

the mystery of the secret passage!"

Paul smiled wearily. "I'll help if you just tell me what we should do."

"Let's ask the professor," Anne suggested. "We'll just say that Rebecca and Paul were in the well and saw that the passageway ends under the house. We could also tell him that we know about the cellar and that we've seen light shining through the cracks. If we keep asking, he'll be forced to answer."

"Forced?" Katie shook her head doubtfully. "To tell us children?"

"Let's invite him to spend an evening in front of the fireplace with us," Anne suggested. "Maybe with Mom here, he'll talk."

Paul and Rebecca had been following the conversation silently. They didn't like the idea of revealing part of their secret. Still they agreed to the plan, hoping to discover something new.

Immediately the children told their mother of their plans. She agreed to inviting Professor Crippen. Since the children were eager to solve the mystery as soon as possible, they decided to invite him for that very evening.

"If it's to be tonight, we'll have to invite him soon," Katie said.

Anne glanced at the clock, "It's eleven o'clock already. The professor usually goes into the passageway around this time. Let's hurry!"

Rebecca turned on the intercom and called the others. "Oh, Anne, why didn't we think of it ten minutes ago? Listen to that!"

They heard the familiar footsteps.

"Too late!" Rebecca wrinkled her brow.

Paul tried to comfort her, "Let's try again in the late afternoon. Maybe he'll come even if the invitation is late."

But that afternoon when the children knocked at Professor Crippen's door, all they heard were the usual sentences on tape. At 7:30 in the evening, they tried one last time, but the response was still the same.

Reinforcement Arrives

Next morning all the children were happy and bustling, because their father would be coming. Mrs. Baker had told him on the phone about their adventures, but he would not have heard all the details. They all hoped he would help them solve their mystery.

"Since the professor is so hard to find," Rebecca reflected, "we should go over now and invite him for the day after tommorow."

Everyone agreed.

Eric knocked, and to the children's disappointment, they heard "Yes?"

"That's strange," Katie murmured. "He never goes to the passageway in the morning. Oh well, we can try again after church, around eleven o'clock."

But at eleven they again heard nothing but the taped message. Three hours later another attempt was also unsuccessful.

At four o'clock the whole family rode to the train station. When the train entered the station, Mrs. Baker and the children eagerly watched the opening doors. Mr. Baker stepped onto the platform and waved cheerfully. Because he was so tall, he could easily look over the heads of the other people.

Tawny was the first to reach his side. People in

the crowd smiled when Mr. Baker hugged his wife and children.

On the ride back the conversation was noisy, with all the children trying to talk at once. "Take it easy!" Mr. Baker cried. "There's plenty of time for you to tell me everything."

An hour later they all sat happily around the dinner table. The children took turns telling everything that had happened during their stay at the castle. Their father was astonished and pleased with what the children had learned.

When Eric told about all the unsuccessful attempts to invite the professor, Mr. Baker's face showed concern. After a moment he told Rebecca to try and invite him for the following evening. "Oh, wait a minute. I'll go with you," he added.

"May I go too?" Eric asked.

The three approached the professor's door and heard the usual sentences on tape. Then silence.

Back at the house, Mr. Baker said, "Well, perhaps he's gone away for a few days."

Paul slipped quietly from the house. He hurried across the courtyard toward the garage. Carefully he tried the door handle. The garage door was locked. Not wanting to give up, he took a closer look at the door and noticed that there were several air slots at the bottom. He bent down, looked through, and saw the professor's car. This meant that Professor Crippen had not driven away in the car.

Back in the living room, Paul reported. "The car is in the garage. The professor must not have taken a trip."

"Good work, Paul." Mr. Baker smiled. "Maybe

we'll find the solution tomorrow."

The Treasure Chest

The next morning the adventures and mysteries were forgotten for a moment as the family made plans for their remaining days at the castle. After a walk the family reentered the courtyard.

"I'd like to tour the castle," Mrs. Baker said. "Let's see if the professor has returned."

But, this time, too, no one opened. Mr. Baker looked at the main building. "Tell me, where do you think the hidden cellar is?"

The children pointed to the part of the wall that projected three feet out of the ground and told about the passageway that led in back of the kitchen fireplace.

"We found a hole in the wall there!" Eric cried, pointing to the crack. When Mr. Baker failed to react, he added, "It must be thirty feet deep."

"Thirty feet?"

"Yes. Come over and take a look."

During all the other excitement the children had completely forgotten the crack in the wall. The children removed the stone and explained that they had found no end to the hole.

Katie went up close and called, "Hello, hello!" She spun around. "Paul," she asked, "did you say something?"

He shook his head.

"You know what I mean — with your ventriloquist voice?" Paul had been experimenting with ventriloquism for several months.

"No," he repeated. "Why?"

"It was as though someone called for help. The voice sounded hollow and high-pitched, like when you do your ventriloquist act."

"You're probably tired," Paul said.

"It sounded like someone calling for help," Katie insisted. "There, did you hear that?"

Everyone stiffened. This time they had clearly heard a call for help coming from the opening.

Anne was the first to react. She stepped up to the hole and called, "Hello!"

"Help!" the answer echoed.

"That was the professor," she whispered. "What are we going to do?"

Everyone looked at Mr. Baker, who stepped forward and called, "Professor Crippen, is it you?"

"Yes, help me!" came the weak reply. "I'm half-buried." His voice trailed off into silence.

Father spun around, "Quick! He seems to be very weak. We have to help him."

"The secret passage starts in the Knights' Hall," Anne cried.

"Come on," Mr. Baker turned to Katie. "Hurry, run and get the key from Mother!"

"What?" she gasped, "We have a key? Since when?"

"I'll explain later," Mr. Baker replied. "Come!"

Katie ran to tell her mother.

"I'll come along," Mrs. Baker said. "I'd like to be in on the adventure too."

Soon they were all in the Knights' Hall. Quickly the children told about the footsteps they had heard on the intercom. Mr. Baker traced this path twice. He remained standing where the three-armed candle holder was hanging. "It must have been here."

First he pressed on every board and molding on the wall paneling. Nothing happened. Then he carefully took hold of the candle holder.

"We've tried that already," Paul said.

"Well," Mr. Baker replied. "What possibilities do we have? Turning to the left, to the right, Hmm, nothing happens."

"Try pushing it to the left or right, up or down," Mrs. Baker suggested.

Mr. Baker tried this, but still nothing happened.

"Try pushing or pulling," she suggested.

When he pulled on the candle holder, it gave way. Startled, he let go for a moment, but began carefully to pull again.

Katie stepped up to the wall and pushed against the panel. It gave way.

"The secret passage!" Eric exclaimed.

The children stared wide-eyed into the long, dismal corridor leading down into the darkness.

"The professor needs our help," Mrs. Baker reminded them.

"But it's so dark in there," Eric gasped.

"We bought the gas lamp for the well," Rebecca exclaimed. "It's in the house. Should I get it?"

Mr. Baker nodded.

"Don't forget the matches," Paul called.

A few minutes later she returned. With trembling hands, Anne lit the lamp. In its bright light they could see that many steps led downward.

"Let's go," Mr. Baker said. "Follow me!"

Their footsteps resounded heavily in the narrow corridor. Damp, moldy air surrounded them.

They had gone twenty or thirty feet down when the passageway widened. Mr. Baker stood still and pointed to a square shaft. At its end, a light was visible.

"If we heard the professor up there, he must be close by," Paul guessed.

"How do we know we're not running into a trap?" Rebecca looked around uncertainly.

Mr. Baker wrinkled his brow. "I can't imagine that. But, we'll soon see. Just in case, Rebecca and Eric will stay here on the stairs. If we run into any danger, you both run up the stairs as fast as you can and call the police."

Both children nodded, relieved to be staying where they were.

"Let's call out once more," Katie suggested. "Hello, professor," she cried, trying to make her voice sound normal.

"Yes, over here," the answer came.

A few yards farther the corridor led into a large room with many pillars and arches. Moisture glistened on the ceiling, and somewhere waterdrops thumped onto the floor. They all stood amazed at this huge underground room. Although the lamp shone brightly and illuminated the farthest corners, the professor was nowhere to be seen.

"Herr Crippen," Mr. Baker called.

"Yes, here." The professor's voice was now more clear and seemed to come from the far corner.

After deciding that Paul should stay and keep watch, the others went forward.

"There, look!" Anne pointed to a hole in the wall with many stones lying in front of it.

Arriving at the opening, Mr. Baker called, "Hello!"

"Yes, here I am," came the distressed answer out of the darkness.

Cautiously Mr. Baker held the lamp up to the opening. The room on the other side was somewhat smaller. In several places stones had been removed from the wall. At one spot there was a larger opening. In front of it lay someone moaning.

Seeing that the room was otherwise empty, Mr. and Mrs. Baker entered, followed by Anne. Drawing near, they saw what happened. Helpless and weak, the professor lay in front of the excavation. Large stones had fallen onto his legs. Because he was lying on his stomach, he had not been able to move away the stones and sand.

Without waiting for an explanation, all three rolled the stones off the professor's body and carefully pulled him out of the sand. Meanwhile the other children had arrived.

"We'll have to call an ambulance," Mrs. Baker said.

In his new position and with the light from the lamp, the professor could look into the recently excavated opening in the wall. With a jolt he sat up, then sank again with a pained expression on his face. "The treasure," he whispered. "The treasure, the treasure!" He stared at the opening and stretched his uninjured arm toward it. Sobbing he whispered again and again, "The treasure, the treasure."

Rebecca gasped, "There's a treasure chest!" The professor covered his face with both hands and cried without restraint.

Mrs. Baker was first to recover from the shock. "Stay here," she said. "I'll run to the apartment and call the ambulance."

"No, no," the professor cried. "Don't bring any strangers down here!"

"Why not?" Mr. Baker asked. "What do you want to hide?"

"Nothing, nothing," Professor Crippen moaned and fell back onto the ground in surrender. "Go ahead and call the ambulance." Suddenly he seemed very old, like a person who had to give up shortly before reaching his goal.

The rest of that day and the next, things happened in rapid succession. After the professor had been brought to the hospital in a nearby town, Herr Martin and two police sergeants arrived to survey the premises. Because no crime had been committed and the discovery was unknown to the public, it was not necessary to block off the location.

The office for the protection of cultural monuments sent an art historian the same day to survey the site. He requested additional experts who would help him retrieve the treasure chest the following day.

Tips for map readers:

The secret cellar rooms are to be found in area Number 18.

The secret passage begins at Number 19 and leads to Number 18.

Professor Crippen and the treasure were found at Number 18.

The well passageway leads from the well to Number 17 and then toward Number 18. Shortly before the "treasure trap," it is filled with gravel and sand.

Uncovering the Secret

T he children were awake early the next morning. The art historian had given them permission to watch him working, and they were eager to be there from the start.

He explained that the professor had overlooked something, and it could have killed him. Only a miracle had saved his life. In the old days traps of all kinds had been built, and the professor had stumbled into one — fortunately, without any great harm.

The historian drew a sketch and explained, "A beam lying on the floor was weighted down with many stones, while another one was laid across a small hole. One top of this beam another one was set upright. This in turn supported the endstone of a ceiling arch. If an unsuspecting person entered the secret passage, he would see various sections of the wall that had been plastered over. If he broke open a certain section, he would upset the delicate balance. The beam, lying out of sight under the pile of debris, would give way under the weight of the arched ceiling. It would be raised up on the other end, and the stone trap would bury the treasure hunter. Probably the professor heard the stones creak, began to run, and thus was injured by only a few stones."

The children listened breathlessly, staring at the mountain of stones that could have crushed the

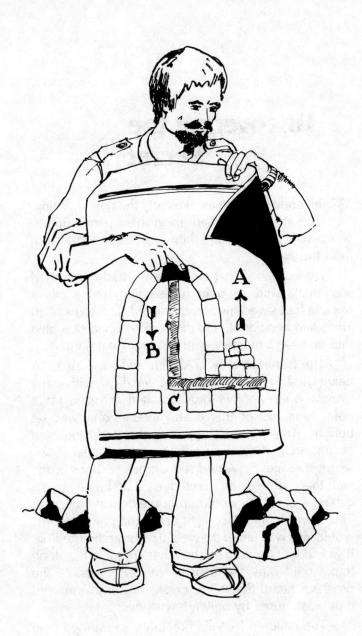

professor.

Cautiously the experts went about their work. Many hours passed before the necessary supports were provided and set in place.

At last the oak chest stood in the cellar room. Because it was large and heavy, it could not be carried out of the cellar. Since no one had a key for the rusty lock, two boards were carefully removed from the bottom.

What then appeared was certainly valuable, but not what the children had expected. Instead of shiny coins and sparkling gems they saw discolored jewelry wrapped in bits of ragged cloth. Not until the art historian pointed out the delicate engraving on the jewelry did they begin to appreciate the contents of the old chest.

"We've found a real treasure!" Rebecca said, her eyes sparkling.

"Yes," the historian said, "You have indeed discovered a valuable treasure." Frowning, he added, "But this seems to be the wealth of just one family. If all the nobles had hidden their valuable possessions here, it would be a much larger amount. The chest would not have been big enough."

"Does that mean the escaping nobles took their valuables with them?" Anne asked.

"It could be."

"But we were told that those people were captured, but their jewelry was not found," Rebecca objected.

"Yes, that's possible," the art historian replied.

"But they might have hidden everything in a different place before leaving," suggested Rebecca.

"Maybe even in the castle?" Eric asked.
The man nodded. "Yes, that is possible."

Another Treasure

The next morning Katie said, "I think it's great that we know about the secret passage and that the treasure has been discovered. But I'm sad, because now all the mystery and adventure of the castle are gone."

The other children nodded. Katie had stated what they all felt. To get their minds off this subject, Mrs. Baker suggested that they make plans for the remaining vacation days. This cheered up everyone, because they wanted to see more of the area. They decided they would first visit the professor in the hospital.

"This evening we have guests," Mrs. Baker announced.

"Guests! Who?" Eric asked.

"Baron von Zerbach has been informed about the discovery and decided to come immediately. Because he'll be living in the castle, I invited him for dinner this evening."

"Great!" Anne said enthusiastically. "I bet he's an interesting person."

At the hospital they found the professor in a room with two other men.

When the family entered, he seemed somewhat embarrassed, but when Mr. Baker greeted him with "God bless you," he answered, "Thank you, and God bless you."

Seeing their surprise, the professor explained. "I grew up in a Christian family. After I received my doctor's degree, I felt empty inside and dissatisfied. When one of my colleagues made a big discovery, I became very jealous. His name became widely known, and everyone read about him in the scholarly journals. But the work I was doing didn't receive any publicity. That's why I searched through old documents and found this castle with its legend of the treasure."

"Well, you did find the treasure," Anne said.

"And you've been interviewed by many reporters," Eric added.

"That's what you were looking for, isn't it?" Katie's questioning eyes were fixed on him.

"Well, yes, but there's still a dark side in my life. Somewhere along the way, the value of the treasure grew more important than fame."

"The value?" Eric asked.

"Yes, I mean the financial value. My addiction to money made me sick."

"I don't understand." Anne shook her head. "You must have known that you couldn't keep the treasure."

Professor Crippen spoke slowly and hesitantly. Everyone in the room sensed that it was difficult for him to talk about his innermost feelings. "Yes, that is the dark side," he continued. "I'm sure that instead of turning the treasure over to the baron, I would have sold the jewelry illegally." The professor drew a deep breath. "If my plans hadn't come to an abrupt end."

"And if we hadn't gotten in your way," Paul said.

"You saved my life. But there is more. When I

was lying there, trapped and in pain, I realized I would not get out without help. I had lots of time to think. During all those lonely hours, I realized that I had been searching for monetary treasures. Because I had a bad conscience, I was running away from the treasure who would have made me really wealthy— Jesus Christ. Because I was afraid no one would find me in this unknown cellar, I began thinking about my past life, asked Christ to forgive my sins, and entrusted my life to Him."

"Did you really think that you wouldn't be found?" Eric asked.

Professor Crippen smiled at the boy. "For a long time I did. My common sense told me that. No one knew where I was, and this cellar was unknown. But then a few hours before you found me, the thought came to me that God can let miracles happen. Before that I hadn't dared to ask, because I felt that this accident was my punishment. But after much prayer, I sensed Jesus' presence. I was free from sin, and I believed in a new future."

"You prayed for help?" Mrs. Baker asked.

The professor nodded. "Yes, even though my common sense told me it was impossible. I said, 'Lord, I'm afraid my life will end here. But if it be your will and you help me get out, I will dedicate the rest of my life to you.'"

Seeing the questioning look in Mrs. Baker's eyes, he explained, "I know that many have bargained with God in hopeless situations and then forgot their promise soon after being helped. When I saw the treasure chest, I felt my old greed returning. But now that's a thing of the past. A friend and former colleague offered me an interesting job in art history, and I've decided to accept. My friend is a dedicated Christian, very active in his church. I'm looking forward to working with him."

The professor's roommates had been listening with great interest. One of them said, "That's great! Something to celebrate!"

Mr. Baker suggested, "Why don't we celebrate by singing our praise to God?"

One song followed another. Finally they all prayed together. Professor Crippen thanked God for being saved and asked God to protect the children and grant them pleasant days for the rest of their vacation at the castle.

When it was time for the family to leave, one of the other patients said, "It's too bad you have to leave. I would like to hear more about this faith."

"Professor Crippen will certainly be able to tell you more," Mr. Baker replied. Turning to the professor, he whispered, "Well, here's your first chance to witness."

Professor Crippen smiled with tears in his eyes. "I've found two treasures—one in the castle and one much more important—Jesus Christ."

The family was so overjoyed that they sang all the way home.

That evening the baron was their guest. When the conversation turned to the secret passage, he said, "It's good that we at least know now where one of them is."

"One?" Paul asked. "Are there more?"

The baron nodded. "There must be at least two more."

"Two more?" asked Katie.

"Yes, two. Your passageway didn't leave the castle. We know that the nobles escaped, despite the siege of the castle. There must have been a passage leading away from the castle."

"And the second one?" Rebecca asked.

"The other one? It sounds strange, but a room exists in this castle which no one has seen for a long time. Five narrow window openings can be seen from the mountain."

"Yes, we saw them too," Katie replied eagerly.

"It's possible to estimate how large the room could be, about 3 x 8 meters. No one has ever entered it, because the entrance is hidden."

"Maybe it's just been walled up," Paul suggested.

"That is possible, but not probable. The fresco paintings on the walls are very old, and they are complete and undamaged. If it has been walled up, then it must have been done five hundred years ago."

The children could hardly wait to experience their next adventure. Seeing their eager faces, the baron added, "So you see, your next project is waiting for you. I would appreciate your finding out the answers to these questions. To enable you to do this," he turned to the parents, "I am extending a permanent invitation to you to visit the castle as long and as often as you wish. The apartment will be available to you at all times."

The children jumped up and down in excitement.

"May we come back again?" Eric asked.

Mr. and Mrs. Baker both nodded in agreement.

Katie exclaimed, "We'll come back again! And we'll have an even more exciting adventure!"